Eva's Way

Trusting God in trial and tragedy

Linda A. Hatinen

ISBN: 1511679034
ISBN 13: 9781511679039

Dedication

This novel is dedicated in memory of Sam Hatinen, my father-in-law, whose mother Eva, is my inspiration for writing. She lost a son during the Cloquet Fire of 1918 while pregnant with my father-in-law, who told me her story with obvious love and gratitude for her and admiration for her Sisu.*

*Sisu—a Finnish word describing the courage, determination and hardiness Finns have demonstrated throughout history

Introduction

Mumo, my grandmother, gave me a set of 12 notebooks and pencils before we left for America. She told me to write down what she had taught me and to also write down our story. She said writing would help me understand as well as be a blessing for our children. I didn't know exactly what she meant about understanding, but I will write. It has been difficult for me to know where to start, but suddenly I remember the morning everything changed...........

1

The Beginning

"And the LORD, He it is that doth go before thee; He will be with thee, He will not fail thee, neither forsake thee: fear not, neither be dismayed."

DEUTERONOMY 31: 8

*I*t was a beautiful February morning, not because it was warm and sunny. I couldn't even see outside from our sleeping partition in the loft, but it was the second Sunday of the month, the only morning my husband and I were spared a predawn rising in order to milk the cows. Though my husband's step-mother Silja had few good points in my estimation, she did believe in the Sabbath as a day of rest, and consequently allowed each married couple abiding on *her land* at least one Sunday monthly free of the milking duties. Today her son Arvo and his wife Margit would be in the barn milking.

Abel, my husband, was tenderly rubbing my swollen belly as he talked just as tenderly to our unborn child. "It won't be much longer little one before you'll have room to stretch your legs. We're waiting for that day."

He smiled broadly, and then bent down to kiss me. He is a wonderful man, and we love each other deeply. What he whispered in my ears I will not write down but carry in my heart forever.

The loving mood was abruptly broken as Abel reached across me, picking up one of his boots from the floor and hurled it at a laughing shape peeking over the curtain separating us from Abel's twelve-year-old twin step-brothers, Antti and Aleski "Perverts!" Abel shouted. "Get out of here before I tan your hides."

If his loud voice or crashing boot hadn't beckoned his step-mother's attention, her darling's ear-piercing scream definitely did. "My nose, my nose, you broke my nose! Ma...."

She climbed the loft ladder faster than I'd ever seen her move, adding to the confusion with her demand of "What have you done to my boys?" Antti's screams were not about to stop and Aleski kept repeating, "He threw his heavy boot right at Antti's head and could have killed him."

"Your darling boys are perverts and deserve more than a boot thrown towards..."

"Shut your mouth, Abel, and help Antti down while I get my medicine bag."

Silja, Abel, Antti and Aleski made it down the ladder just as my father-in-law came through the door. "Eero, your son has gone way to far this time. As soon as the baby comes, they're out of here!" Silja spat out angrily.

"Settle down, Silja, and tell me what happened to Antti." I stayed in the loft, listening intently, but not wanting to even be near Silja in one of her angry moods. My mother always said Silja could curdle milk just by looking at it, and I did not want to tangle with her.

Eero's calm voice settled down the boys, and somehow he convinced Silja to go rest. Abel was calm also as I heard him explain what had happened. "The boys were peeking over the curtains again. We have no privacy, and I threw a boot at them which hit Antti's nose. Pa, things can't go on like this. It's not good for any of us. Remember I still have my Army pay—enough to build a little cottage in the field. We don't need much."

Eero whispered a response I couldn't hear, but I got the impression he was in agreement. I did hear him tell Abel that they would talk in the barn later.

The tension in the house was thick and heavy. Silja stayed in her bed, sickened with a headache, so I was left with the kitchen chores, cleaning up the forgotten breakfast, making dinner and supper. The twins seemed none the worse for wear, except for being quiet, as they were in and out of the kitchen for meals.

Arvo and Margit knew something was wrong, but they didn't ask any questions at first. They came in after milking and helped themselves to breakfast and also joined us for dinner and supper. They left immediately after dinner, but seemed in no hurry after supper. Margit, uncharacteristically, even offered to help clean up the kitchen, and after a busy—and tense—day, I gratefully accepted her help. It became obvious that Margit had an ulterior motive—finding out what was going on. "What's wrong with Silja?" she asked.

"I don't really know, but I think she has a bad headache."

"Eero seemed really quiet too."

"He's probably worried about her."

I was surprised I could be so vague to such direct questions but felt uneasy about confiding in Margit. I liked her all right but didn't know her well. I felt badly we had conceived a baby before she and Arvo had, and I wondered if she was worried they would have to give up their little cottage in the field for us. Perhaps that was what Eero and Abel were talking about.

With the large kitchen spotless and Arvo and Margit having gone back to their cottage, I was sitting at the table, darning socks, when the door quietly opened. Abel, with a flushed face, whispered, "Eva, come to the barn. Pa wants you to hear this too." With no inkling of what I was to hear, but extremely curious, I followed my husband to the barn into the tack room, where the leather work is done.

Eero was sitting on a bale of hay but got up quickly to make room for me. "Thank you for doing so much extra work today, Eva, to cover for Silja. You're a wonderful help."

"Abel, shut the door, please. I don't want any stray ears. Eva, thank you for coming to the barn to hear me out. Abel and I have been doing lots of talking as we worked today, and I know he will fill you in on whatever I omit due to my poor memory."

He looked up at the rafters then, and unless I was mistaken there were tears in his eyes. A man of great kindness but few words, he began the longest discourse I had ever heard from him:

"Abel's mother and I grew up in the village, which you no doubt know. Her father was the Lutheran pastor, a good man raising his youngest daughter alone since his wife had died along with their seventh child. His other children were older and had all moved to Helsinki to find work. I became the handyman/gardener for the church just like my father had been before his joints refused to do the work.

"Anyway Liisa and I loved each other from a young age, and her father generously allowed me to marry her even though I was of a lower class. I had nothing but an able body and love for his daughter, but he said along with my faith in God that was enough. He married us and allowed us to live in the gardener's house. He was proud of how Liisa fixed it up and seemed pleased to see her happily married. He shared what he had with us and even gave Liisa most of her mother's belongings. I don't know what his other children thought of that, but it's what he chose to do. He said that Liisa reminded him of her mother, and he wanted her to have the things that she had treasured.

"For two years we could not have been happier. When Abel was born, we felt very blessed. Abel was just a few days short of a year when our second baby died along with Liisa. If only we hadn't been so hungry for each other..."

He paused for a while but finally continued, "Her father had no problem with Abel and me continuing to live in the cottage, and I appreciated that. Liisa's father and I were two broken-hearted men. The only one who kept us going, Abel, was you. The housekeeper watched you while I did the outside work, and before long we were living in the main house with the pastor. He talked a lot about grieving, our eternal soul, and the saving grace of Jesus, and I finally passed the corner where I believed I could survive.

"Just as my life was falling into a rhythm, though a shaky one, the old pastor died, and the church was closed. The bishop himself told me I was no longer welcome, making matters worse by accusing me of taking advantage of the old pastor.

"I packed a rucksack of our few belongings, most importantly a wooden box containing the jewelry and trinkets given to Liisa by her father. I knew I'd be officially charged with theft if I were found with the jewelry, so I walked many, many miles, mostly through the woods until by accident, or divine intervention, I ended up at Silja's. I didn't trust anyone, so I hid the wooden box in this very room and slept here.   I planned to leave in the morning, but exhausted, I overslept, so we couldn't sneak out. Instead, Silja came into the barn with a little tot and discovered us. When she learned of the loss of your mother and our home, she offered a cot in the barn and meals in exchange for my labor.

"My father had died, and we had no other offers, so, of course, we stayed. Eventually I learned that the little guy was really a year older than you, Abel, and that Silja's husband had been killed in a hunting accident. She was as alone as I was, but she had land and a large house and a large herd of livestock. For almost a year, we kept our distance. You stayed right beside me, and we ate food that was placed in the barn. Then, one day you and Arvo discovered each other. With both of you starved for the company of other children, you ran and chased each other, laughing and chattering. I realized how good each of you was for the other, and was pleased when Silja noticed the same. We were in the house for the first time when Silja invited us for Arvo's name day celebration.   I had whittled a horse for a gift, but when I saw the extravagant gifts Silja had purchased for Arvo, I kept the horse in my pocket.

"A few weeks later she invited us to eat inside on a regular basis, and then one night she shocked me by saying she'd been thinking how foolish it was for the two of us to be staying in the barn when she had so much space. I'll never forget how she looked at me—like a horse she was think-ing of buying.

"She was always direct, and one evening weeks into our new arrange-ment, she said, 'I suppose it wouldn't be so bad to have another child. We have to wed though.' And that's what happened. To be honest, she was good to both you and me for all of ten years. I'd been loved once and didn't even expect it to happen again. To know that you'd have what you needed was plenty for me. She was decent to you until the twins arrived, and then things fell apart.   Everything revolved around her boys. Oh, I know they're mine too, but somehow...oh, I'm saying way too much.

Anyway, she didn't enjoy mothering twins. Aleski was very colicky, and you, Abel, were the best at comforting him. You'd carry him around, holding him tightly against you—even in the middle of the night. To be truthful, you and I both cared for the twins until something became very apparent. Abel, you were the capable son Silja would have loved to have had, and Arvo didn't seem to have a whit of common sense. He was a dreamer and story teller, and he still is. He's not a bad man, but he's not interested in farming or work in general. She did everything she could for him, including having the cottage built for him and Margit. Now she's bitter that they have no children and even more bitter that he has so little interest in the farm. She has enough land to have ten more cottages built, but when I suggested one for the two of you, she wouldn't hear of it, saying she wouldn't give up any more land. I think it's more of not being able to handle the comparison of you with Arvo. Now she gets angry any time she sees you alongside him. She's never said it, but I think she's worried that the twins are turning out lazy too. She never wanted me to make them work, so I finally gave up, something I'm not proud of.

"That was a round about way of getting to my point: I've known for a long time that you probably wouldn't be able to stay here permanently. Nor did I think you'd ever want to. If you're willing, I might have a solution. You no doubt know that America is huge and eager for settlers. They'll even give you land to keep if you'll stay and farm it." He looked at us with hopeful eyes.

I knew it wasn't my position to ask, but I did: "Abel, how can we? Our baby is coming soon. Surely you want him to be born here, and it would be hard to travel with a toddler."

Abel had obviously talked about this at length with his father, and I could see the eagerness in his eyes, as he responded: "Thousands of Finns have left for America, and more are leaving all of the time. There's just not enough land here. We'd have a chance for a good start—for the three of us. I can't deny I've thought about it often but could never figure out how we could afford passage." Abel opened the door to look around, and then whispered, "But the miracle is that Pa wants to help us. Tell her, Pa."

"I already told you that Liisa's father gave her jewelry and baubles that had belonged to her mother. What I didn't tell you is that I never told Silja about them. I always felt that Liisa's son and his wife should have them. Now I know it was the right thing to do. I'm sure we can sell them for enough money to buy passage to America. They'll stay hidden until you want to leave. Now go in, and think about it, but stay quiet."

I was speechless. I knew people who had gone to America, but they never came back to tell us anything about it. I needed to talk with Abel, but somehow felt the decision had already been made. I badly needed to talk with my parents, and especially with Mumo....and that's what I would do on Tuesday, the day that had already been set aside—and most importantly—cleared with Silja.......

2

Unspoken Questions

"The LORD is good, a strong hold in the day of trouble; and He knoweth them that trust in Him."

NAHUM 1:7

The next day was one of the most difficult I had ever experienced. I desperately wanted to talk with Abel, but every time I started to, he put his finger to his lips, gesturing me to be quiet. So, instead of sharing my concerns, I imagined great hardships as I milked the cows, glad I could do it without having to see, as my eyes continually filled with tears.

The kitchen work with Silja was the worst. I had trouble concentrating, and she was as cross as a bear. Her "Get with it, Eva. You're as slow as Margit today" only made me feel worse, but somehow breakfast was prepared, and I filled bowls with oatmeal and poured cups of coffee.

The twins came down, and I couldn't help but notice Antti's eyes and nose were black and blue. Silja took one look at him, and her anger flared as she stared at Abel.

As usual, Arvo and Margit were the last ones in from the barn, and as he sat down, Arvo looked at Antti and said, "So who were you in a fight with, little man?"

Antti didn't know what to answer and turned bright red. Eero saved the day by saying "He put his nose where it didn't belong and collided with a shoe."

"I think I'm missing part of the story, so I'll make up my own, Eero replied. "Once there was a skinny Finn, who liked to ski. One day..."

"Stop it," said Silja, "No wonder I get headaches." The rest of our meal was eaten in silence until Arvo asked, "Pa, could Margit and me ride into town with you tomorrow?"

"Sorry, Arvo, but I'll have a full wagon with the milk, Abel and Eva and the twins." I didn't know why Eero was taking the twins, who usually skied to school, but I was sure Eero had his reasons.

Silja added, "I need you and Margit here for cheese making tomorrow at least by seven. That way we'll be done by noon."

"What about milking?" asked Margit.

"Abel and Eva, Eero and I will take care of that this time. I'll put the pots of water on before I go to the barn, and then you can put the jars of cream in as soon as you come."

"Will do," said Margit, unable to hide her delight at not having to milk cows. She wasn't very good at it and obviously disliked the work.

Silja hugged the boys as she handed them their lunch pails, ignored Eero and Abel, and reminded Arvo and Margit once again not to be late in the morning.

That left me to clean up the breakfast dishes while Silja put on tubs of water for doing laundry. Soon the kitchen was humid with the simmering water. We had a good routine for doing laundry. Everyone put their dirty clothes in a big basket in the kitchen on Sunday evening or Monday morning. Silja did the scrubbing while I rinsed them and cranked them through the wooden wringers, removing as much water as possible. I'd then hang the clothes from the lines outside or, in the winter, from the ones that were set up in the basement. I struggled greatly going down the stone steps with the basket but dared not complain. Once in the basement I appreciated the quiet. By the time I got back to the kitchen, Silja was done washing and had even rinsed and wrung out the last load. I knew she would make a comment about my being slow, so was not surprised when she said, "It looks like you can't keep up with this job either."

Normally, I would have said nothing, but I blurted out, "I have a hard time carrying the basket down the steps. That must have slowed me down."

"Yah, and just for your information I went up and down those same stairs when I was carrying twins. You young folks are spoiled. That's the problem."

I held my tongue and did my work all the while hearing Silja mumble to herself about how hard she had it. I scrubbed the floor after doing laundry, my usual job, because there always seemed to be splattered water from doing laundry. The kitchen is the biggest room in the house, and it took me a long time. Abel came in as I was finishing and offered to dump the water tubs and buckets out for me, which I appreciated. By then my back hurt, and I knew I had to rest a bit. As soon as I sat down,

Silja came into the kitchen to start lunch and said, "It must be nice to have so much time on your hands."

I repeated Philippians 2:14 to myself, grateful Mumo had encouraged me to memorize so many Bible verses. I got up and helped with dinner, washed dishes and started supper before I was finally able to lie down for a few minutes. Somehow after that short rest I made it through the rest of the day, all the while eagerly waiting for bedtime.

Morning came quickly, but that was fine with me because I'd have a day of respite. The cow milking and breakfast went smoothly, and we were off in the wagon by seven. As we left, Silja told Eero to stop at Arvo and Margit's since they hadn't shown up yet. He said he would, and we loaded up into the wagon covering ourselves with quilts.

It didn't take long for me to understand why Eero had offered a ride to the boys. Before we even started, he told Antti and Aleski to apologize to us for spying. They said a reluctant sorry, and Eero said, "Notice I didn't ask Abel to apologize to you. You deserved what you got and then some."

I was surprised to hear Eero speak so harshly, and I must admit it pleased me to see the twins put their heads down, unable to look at any of us. With that done, the ride to Arvo's cottage went quickly, and Abel got down from the wagon. I saw him knock on the door but get no answer. He asked me to go in just in case Margit wasn't dressed. I did as he asked, knocking once more and then opening the door. I was shocked to see Margit coming out of their bedroom, wrapped in a blanket, obviously having just been roused from sleep. When I reminded her Silja was waiting for them, she cursed and said "Arvo, we're late to help your mother. Get up."

I heard Arvo mumble something, and then I left but could not help notice the disarray in what I had thought was such a cozy cottage. Dirty dishes were still on the table along with empty wine bottles, and clothing was strewn throughout the room. I was relieved to leave and to tell Abel and Eero that they'd overslept.

With obvious concern, Eero said, "Well, they'll have to sort it out with Silja," and with that we left. The way to my home was short. Abel and my homes were separated only by Silja's fields. I thought back to growing up, watching Abel work in the fields, having a crush on the big, strong man who didn't even notice me, a little girl five years younger than him.

When he came back from serving in the Russian Army, I had grown up and he not only noticed me but asked my father for my hand in marriage. Permission was given, banns posted, and six months later, after a wonderful courtship, we were married. Here I was 10 months later, at 19, married and about to have our first baby.

We came to the familiar driveway, and I admired the birch trees alongside it. Then the house in which I'd grown up came into view, and I smiled at the little yellow building with green shutters. It looked happy even from the outside. It was funny; I seemed to be seeing things differently, knowing I probably would be here for only another year or so...............

3

Unconditional Love

"Beloved, if God so loved us, we ought to love one another."

I JOHN 4:11

She must have been watching for me, since before I even touched it, the door was opened by my mother. She still wore her kerchief over her hair, so she couldn't have been in from the barn for long. "Come in, come in, child," she purred as she pulled me into a big hug. We entered a small, enclosed porch that held the aroma of smoked meats and drying herbs, and then as she opened the door to the kitchen, I felt the wonderful familiarity of happiness and love that I never realized how badly I missed until I was immersed in it once again.

Greetings were exchanged, my coat hung up, my growing stomach was admired, and then we three generations of women sat down to steaming mugs of hot coffee and fresh pulla (a braided sweet yeast bread flavored with cardamom). "You must have been up early Mumo, the bread is still warm-- and delicious."

She always made me feel as if I were the most special person in the world, and did so again, as she looked into my eyes, and said, "I set it last night but baked it this morning, so it would be fresh."

"We want you to keep coming," my mother added.

It must have been my pregnancy or the stress of the last few days because those few words shook me to the core, and tears spilled down my cheeks as I told them all that had been happening. My mother and grandmother just let me pour out my concerns, which was probably just what I needed.

When I heard the door open several minutes later, I looked up with red, swollen eyes to see my father, who said, "So did the world come to an end while I was finishing up?"

"Shush, Pa," my mother scolded. Eva has had to put up with the wicked witch, and telling about it brought some good, cleansing tears."

"Oh, Pa, I have worse news. I think we are going to America." My family was quiet, a trait seldom practiced when we were together. Pa finally broke the silence by saying, "I can't say that makes me happy, but I'm not exactly surprised. When Abel asked for your hand, it was obvious he had ambition, and that it involved farming. Of course, he wants land, and it won't happen in Finland. We're losing lots of our fine young folks to America, but I can't say I blame them."

I could not stop my tears from flowing as I told the naked truth: "It scares me. I don't want to leave."

"Have you told Abel how you feel?" asked Ma.

"No."

"Smart girl," Mumo said. "You don't want to get between your man and his dreams."

Those words brought more tears, but then Pa, with his usual practical approach to life said, "It's time for the tears to stop. You're a strong girl. You're a Finn, and you have plenty of Sisu. That's the way you were raised, and don't ever forget it. Now I'm going to do my chores. When the time gets closer to your leaving, be sure to bring Abel over. I know I have tools I can spare."

Mumo and Ma didn't say a word until Pa had left, and then they bombarded me with questions for which I had no answers. I finally had to tell them that I'd had no chance to talk to Abel but that I would on the way home.

Mumo, who was not only my grandmother and mentor, but my midwife, moved the conversation to the baby, which was a relief. She asked me many questions about how I felt, and continually nodded reassuringly. After examining me, she announced, "It looks to me like you have six weeks left at the most, and these are important weeks for both of you. Baby is growing and getting stronger, especially in his lungs. You need to keep well rested and relaxed. When the wicked witch bothers you, just imagine her with a long nose and warts. It will make you want to laugh instead of cry, which just wears you out." We both laughed at that picture and how puzzled Silja would be. After we quit laughing, she told me we would start talking about what to expect during labor and delivery, and that's exactly what we did. An hour or two later she asked if I had any questions.

"Just one, Mumo. Will it be safe for me to climb up and down the ladder to the loft with the baby in my arms? How should I do it?"

"Don't tell me you and Abel are still in the loft. It won't be safe when the baby's here, and it isn't safe *now*. Unless Silja shows a whit of common sense and allows you to move downstairs, you need to stay here until the baby's born. In fact, don't even ask about moving from the loft. I want you here. You tell Silja your midwife will have it no other way." Her words made me chuckle—as if Silja would listen to her. In fact, we three women laughed and laughed—perhaps all for different reasons-- but also with a shared joy of knowing we cared for one and another. Once we had wiped happy tears from our eyes, Mumo ended her midwife session with her usual prayer:

> *Heavenly Father, it was you who told us to be fruitful and multiply. Protect the baby growing in Eva's womb. Keep him or her well. Prepare Eva's body and mind for birthing and mine for assisting her.*
>
> *In Jesus Name,*
> Amen

The rest of the morning and afternoon was light-hearted, full of talking and laughter. When Pa came in for lunch he announced "Ah, all is well in my world. My girls are laughing again."

Sooner than I was ready, Abel and Eero arrived. Almost before they had entered the door, Mumo announced, "It's time for Eva to move here. The baby's arrival is just weeks away, and she can't be climbing the ladder to a loft. I want her close by to keep my eyes on her and the baby."

The men were surprised but weren't about to question Mumo's authority. After all, she'd birthed most of the babies, including Arvo and the twins, in the parish during the past 30 years.

"We'll drop her and her things off next Tuesday if that's soon enough."

"Yah, but no later, and sooner would be better," Mumo replied.

And that's how it happened that I spent the last weeks of my pregnancy with my family. When I look back, it was a blessed time, preparing me for much of my journey. But I'm getting ahead of myself.

We returned to Silja's, and as usual my optimism made me believe she would have softened in the time we were gone. But no such miracle had occurred. Rather she was fit to be tied as we hung up our clothes and put the wagon quilts away. The kitchen was far from its usual tidiness, and Silja immediately started throwing out orders while she complained about her day:

"Abel, carry the cheese out to the milk house. Eva, get the pots washed while I finish the soup. Eero, I can't help with milking tonight. I've been working alone all day. Why didn't you tell Arvo and Margit to get their lazy bodies here?"

"We did tell them. They were still in bed when we arrived but said they'd come. We believed them," said Eero. I was surprised and relieved that he shared the blame with me, not indicating I was the only one who had entered the cottage.

The afternoon somehow passed with me cleaning up from the cheese-making, finishing making our supper and milking once again. Silja disappeared to her bed, but not before I heard Eero telling her I would be staying with my family. "Ridiculous," she replied. "The princess is just trying to get out of work" was the last thing I heard her say before she slammed the bedroom door shut.

Silja was not going to change, but I was comforted, knowing that I would be with my family until the baby arrived, and that we'd leave permanently in a year or so.   As much as I didn't want to leave my family, I wanted more to be away from Silja and her anger.

4

Waiting

"Bless them who persecute you: bless, and curse not."

ROMANS 12:14

The following week passed very slowly. Silja was not only angry but very resentful, continually conveying how hard she worked and how undeserving everyone else was. She could not get over that not only had Arvo and Margit not shown up to help her make cheese, but that they seemed without remorse. Most of the time when they were on the farm, they appeared silly and care-free. Abel had come to the conclusion that they fortified themselves with liquor before appearing at the farm. Whatever the case, Silja must have been amazed that she had so little control over them. They didn't even stay for meals any more, which actually was somewhat of a relief.

The males of the family simply stayed away from Silja, giving her little opportunity to vent to them. But I continued to work beside her, assisting with most of the kitchen work, laundry, and cleaning. She found fault with everything I did, and frequently told me there was absolutely no reason for my leaving the farm just because I was pregnant. One day I courageously told her I didn't feel safe using the loft ladder, and she simply scoffed at me, saying that was a poor excuse that could have been simply solved had I but asked.

Abel and I finally found opportunities to talk, and it was obvious he was very excited about the prospect of leaving for America. He and his father talked frequently, and Eero was glad to be of assistance to us. He had told Abel that helping us made him feel young and hopeful again. They had figured out costs for passage and even getting started in America, and Eero felt able to fully fund those activities. He told Abel he had sweated blood and tears for his Army money, so he should put it aside for a rainy day.

Abel had talked to many men at market and learned that thousands of Finns were settling in Michigan and Minnesota. There was mining and farming in both regions, and supposedly lots of water also. Abel's eyes lit up when he started talking about "our farm" and the land available for crops. He told me his father had made a large wooden trunk for us that even had a lock, and that they would begin filling it with things we would need. He even suggested that while I'd be at my parents' house I could see if they had extra "womanly" things for us.

I remember one of the days when Abel said, "It's beginning to seem possible. Our dream can come true." I held my tongue and did not remind him it was his dream, not mine. What would have been the use?

On Monday night, the night before I was leaving, Arvo and Margit came for supper. I don't know if someone had invited them or if they came on their own, but they seemed ready for a party. They brought bottles of homemade wine with them, which they poured for all. "The next time we see you, you'll be parents,"Arvo said to Abel and me, "so for tonight we toast living without responsibility. To the easy life!" They lifted their glasses and clinked them together. Arvo and Margit drank glass after glass of their wine, oblivious to how shocked the rest of us were. When they left, I was glad. After cleaning the kitchen, I put my few belongings in the satchel I had used when I moved into Silja's house. I would miss Abel but was still overjoyed to be escaping Silja's wrath.

— —

The next morning after milking, I hung up my kerchief and apron and ate breakfast hurriedly. "You can hardly wait to leave, can you?" sneered Silja. There was no good way to answer, so I said nothing. "Well, I don't envy you with your narrow hips. You'll be lucky if you even survive childbirth. Just remember both Abel's grandmother and mother died giving birth, and I'm *not* going to take care of another motherless child."

I turned my back, nodded to Abel, and went outside where I would wait until the men were ready. I had known Silja was an angry woman, but I hadn't believed before that moment that she was truly evil. I was more than ready to leave.

5

Mumo's School

"The aged women, that they be in behaviour as becometh holiness, not false accusers, not given to much wine, teachers of good things; That they may teach the young women to be sober, to love their husbands, to love their children..."

TITUS 2:3, 4

"I am sorry you have to leave, but I know it's best for you and baby," said Abel as he joined me outside. "She sure revealed her true spirit today"

"And I am sorry you have to stay," I replied. "I don't know how your father stands her."

"I don't either. But he'll survive. And we'll make a good home and fill it with children. They will be blessed to have you for a mother."

"And you for their father." We snuggled close together, enjoying the beautiful morning, each other, and the peace.

"I won't be far away, you know. You'll come visit, won't you?'

"You couldn't keep me away, Eva. I'll see you every Sunday. I've already talked to Pa about it, and he said he wouldn't have it any other way."

"He's a kind man."

"Yes, and I appreciate him more now than ever."

"Do you think we'll ever return to Finland?"

"Truthfully, I must say no. If things go as I anticipate, we'll be very busy developing our farm and home. Besides you'll have so many children you'll never want to leave."

"Who said anything about leaving our babies? I'd take them all with—and you, too."

"I'm so glad I'd be included. I thank you, Eva, for thinking of me."

"After our *first* baby is born, I don't want to be parted from you ever again."

"You have a deal, my lovely wife, but I trust we should seal it with a kiss." And we did.

— ~

The ride to my parents' home was quickly over. Abel carried my satchel, and we entered the house, hanging up our coats and arriving in the kitchen with rosy cheeks and happy smiles.

"You two look happy," said Ma. "We haven't seen enough of you late-ly, Abel."

"Am I even welcome here knowing I'm taking your daughter and grandchild away?"

"You are more than welcome. We've talked lots since hearing your news, and we know you're making a difficult but good decision. You just promise you'll take good care of our little girl and the many babies the two of you will have."

"You have my solemn vow," Abel said so seriously that tears came to my eyes.

"Then you will go with our blessings and prayers," my mother re-plied, "and now let's have some coffee."

With coffee and pulla we visited until Pa invited Abel to the barn to look over some tools he had set aside for him. When they returned to the house Abel was grinning, telling all of us how generous my father was and how much he appreciated the tools. "That reminds me," Mumo said, "I have put some things aside also." She disappeared to her room returning with a bulky bundle that was wrapped with oilcloth. "I have samples of many seeds here, Eva, for you to plant. There are also herbs and spices and 12 notebooks and pencils."

I had no idea what she was talking about until she took a small brown notebook from her apron pocket, saying, "I kept one out just in case you want to start taking some notes. I have lots to teach you while you're here."

"And I better leave, so school can began," joked Abel, as he hugged me good-bye, took Mumo's package, and was on his way.

The truth of the matter was that in the next few weeks, I learned a great deal, and my notebook was always at hand to enter the information and wisdom Mumo and my parents shared with me.

When I asked Ma where she wanted me to put my satchel, she told me Mumo had requested I stay in her room. When I brought my satchel in, I found out Mumo had added a cot to her already crowded room "in case you need the whole bed." She continually amazed me with her giving spirit.

As I walked through my birth home, I once again experienced seeing everything with new eyes. I had always loved this little home, but now, as I compared it with Silja's much grander house, I realized what made it unique and lovely. It was a house of order, comfort and beauty. Now I knew those things didn't come without someone intentionally making it so. The house vividly reflected the beliefs and priorities of the people living in it.

I noticed the little touches all around, bringing warmth and coziness. At meals, the table was carefully set and almost always had a centerpiece of flowers, whether fresh or dry, or a plant. Pa sometimes said he lived in a jungle, but I believe he was secretly proud of what his wife and mother could grow. The food was usually simple but tasty and beautiful. Ma did not have many special plates or dishes, but what she had she used often. It made me realize that everyone who sat at my parents' table must have felt cared for and important.

I knew that Silja's house had many more rooms than my family's home, but I much preferred our little house. I tried to figure out the differences. Both families were Finnish. Both families possessed Sisu. And both families were Christian. The clearest way I could express the differences was that our family home was filled with love, and the love impacted everything.

"Mumo's School" started that very day as she first showed me her own collection of notebooks that she had filled all through her adulthood. There must have been 50 books, filled with her neat handwriting and drawings. As she showed them to me, she told me that I should write often about my life, especially about motherhood and my spiritual life, and even about things that confused me. Mumo said, "Someday your writing will be a blessing to your children, but while you do it, writing always helps you understand." I wasn't sure what she meant, but I was sure to write down what she said and found myself thinking about its meaning often.

For me, during those "school weeks," I jotted down recipes, directions, advice, and stories that I was told. Mumo often referred to Bible verses as she talked. I had never before realized how her ideas about life were so strongly based on her belief in God. One day she said, "God made this wonderful world, and he gave us amazing minds and bodies. If we take care of and use what he gave us, we will be blessed."

Ma was kitchen-oriented. She let me look through her recipes (that I didn't even know she had) and copy any I wanted. Each day I wrote in my little notebook five or six of them. Better yet, as she cooked and I helped her, she showed me little tricks that she used. I realized I had only been an assistant when it came to cooking. I was excited to eventually have my own home where I would be in charge of meals.

I wrote down some of Ma's quotes too. One day she said, "You have a good man, but there will be days when it's hard to be kind and loving to him. Do it anyway." She also said, "The years raising children are very busy, but should be savored. They'll go fast, and you can never have them back."

Even Pa gave me advice. He told me, "Farming isn't easy, but it's a good life. Take care of your children and the house and don't complain. That way Abel won't have to worry about you and how you're doing. Whatever you can do to help will be appreciated."

Mumo and my parents all talked about farming and contributed their own viewpoint. Pa gave me lots of information about crops and taking care of hens and sheep. He talked about the "joy" of harvest time, but later Ma told me it can be an overwhelming time. Mumo chimed in, "Plan ahead. Keep everything else simple during the fall of the year, and thank God for everything that ripens."

Mumo gave me many tips for caring for children also. One of her favorite tips was the use of lanolin for dry skin and for a baby's bottom. She told me to even use it on my nipples when I first started to breast feed. She said because of the many uses for lanolin, we should always raise a few sheep. She talked about many things I'd never thought of, from treating fevers to nutrition and sanitation. As my notebook filled, my heart filled also—with love and appreciation.

6

The Arrival

"Lo, children are a heritage of the LORD, and the fruit of the womb is His reward."

PSALMS 127:3

On a bright Sunday morning in March, four weeks after I'd arrived, my water broke, and within an hour I'd begun labor. I was surprised that the pains were mild, but Mumo warned they would get stronger as time went on. She prepared a cot for me in the sauna dressing room, which was still warm from its use the previous night. "Finns often begin labor after a sauna," Mumo explained. "The heat and steam relax your body. It's a good preparation." She kept a small fire going in the stove, keeping the temperature just warm enough. Between pains, she encouraged me to walk. "You're not sick, so there's no need to be in bed." At one point I needed to throw up and felt better afterward.

Mumo told me she hoped I could deliver in the sauna, which had a set of three tiered benches. She told me I'd sit on the middle one and lean against the highest bench. It sounded very uncomfortable until I saw the pillows she'd put in the sauna, padding the benches. "When you start pushing, I'll be on the bottom bench ready to help the baby." She explained that the cot was in the dressing room if and when I became worn out and for after the baby was born. She had a basket of equipment with her, but nothing looked very scary. There was a pan, wash cloths, a blanket, string, and a knife. She boiled water on the sauna stove and dipped the knife in to kill the germs and then lined up her tools on the bench. Then she said I should remove my skirt, shirt, shoes and socks. She gave me soap and a cloth to wash myself while she brought my folded clothes to the dressing room. When she returned I noticed she had rolled up her sleeves and put on a clean, but badly stained apron. She hummed hymns as she gave me water to drink and then said, "Birthing is usually messy. The sauna's the perfect place for it. I've heard there are doctors delivering some babies, and they insist the mothers deliver while in bed. It makes no sense to me."

I thought of everything Mumo had taught me over the past weeks and did my best to relax and to breathe through the pains. She told me to focus on one of the sauna rocks, and though it sounded silly, it seemed to help. I'd see Mumo close her eyes from time to time and knew she was praying.

Hours later the pains were coming right on top of each other, and I felt overwhelmed. Mumo told me the baby would be coming soon. She helped me remove my shift, got me settled on the bench, and wiped off my forehead and face with cool water. All the time she kept saying soothing words and humming hymns.

She examined me and said, "When you feel the need to push, go right ahead, and God be with you." After I'd pushed for a while she told me she saw the head. "You're doing great. Just a few more strong pushes."

And after three more hard pushes I had the amazing sensation of feeling the baby leave my body. I was laughing and crying as Mumo put the baby on my belly. "We're not quite done, but meet your son."

I was fascinated with my little boy as I listened to his healthy cry. Mumo was cleaning me off, and then I felt the need to push once again. "Here comes the placenta, an absolute miracle." I wasn't impressed and resented the interruption as she showed me the placenta and raised it above my belly to allow the last sharing of blood from my body with my son. Then she deftly tied the umbilical cord in two places and made a cut in between. Suddenly I started shivering violently, and she covered me with a blanket. Then she wrapped the baby tightly in cloths and a small blanket, the same one I'd been wrapped in nineteen years earlier she told me, and handed him to me.

Mumo had given me many instructions, so I knew to touch the baby's cheek encouraging him to turn towards my nipple, which I pressed between my fingers to flatten. He grasped it tightly in his mouth and began to suckle. I knew my milk wouldn't come in for a day or two, but Mumo had told me the first food (I think she called it colostrum) was very important to the baby. After what seemed like only a few minutes, she told me I should switch him to the other breast, which I did. I was amazed at how beautiful my baby was. I hadn't known I'd be fascinated by the swirls in his hair, by his mouth, and by his beautiful fingers and toes. He fell asleep while he was nursing, but I couldn't put him down. Mumo put a shawl around my shoulders and asked if I wanted to lie down. I suddenly realized I was very tired and gratefully lay down on the cot. My little boy fit beautifully in the crook of my arm, and Mumo covered us with a warm quilt.

"I'm going to go tell your parents they have a grandson, and then I'll come back to check on you two. Sleep if you can. You worked hard and did very well."

"Thank you Mumo for everything. I couldn't have done it without you."

"Yes you could. And thank the good Lord for everything." And I did.

7

Welcomes & Farewells

"But the fruit of the Spirit is love, joy, peace, longsuffering, gentleness, goodness, faith, meekness, temperance; against such there is no law."

GALATIANS 5:22

The next few weeks were about as fun as any could be. Abel came hours after our baby was born. He was thrilled to be a father. He held our little boy so reverently that I teared up—again. Together we looked at his little body, admiring his perfection from head to toe. Abel kept saying, "He's so little and so perfect." I completely agreed with him. It was obvious he did not want to leave when our time together came to an end. Ma told him that Pa, Mumo, and she would take good care of baby and me. Just as he was leaving we realized we hadn't even talked about a name. Ma assured us that he could be "baby" until his christening.

I felt like a queen as my family kept checking on how baby and I were doing. Monday morning was very eventful. The black stool, Mumo was waiting for the baby to pass, arrived. She said it came from the co-lostrum, and now that it had come through, I could switch to the soft, woolen nappies that were much more absorbent than the cloths I'd been using. She cleaned him up telling me she'd used oil since the first stool was very sticky. That was another tidbit to write in my notebooks under childcare. The second event was that my milk came in. When I heard the baby cry, I experienced the unique sensation of the letdown, for which Mumo had prepared me. It was a miracle to experience milk dripping from my breasts. Baby was an enthusiastic nurser, and I was relieved to know he was receiving nourishment from me. Mumo showed me tricks to burp him, and we both laughed when he let out a loud burp.

I felt wonderful and realized I was totally in love with our little boy. Abel came every day, often bringing members of his family with him. Eero was excited, claiming the baby gave him a whole new motivation to live and to help us as much as he could. He said the baby looked a lot like Abel when he had been born, and both he and Abel seemed proud about that. When the twins stopped on their way home from school, they were not as impressed with the baby as with the hot chocolate and pulla Mumo gave them. They did ask when I'd be coming back, saying there was way too much work to do, as they reluctantly left the warm kitchen.

Arvo and Margit came with Abel. Margit admired the baby while Arvo appeared uncomfortable. The most surprising visit was the one I dreaded, that of Silja. She could not have been nicer, though, asking if she could hold the baby and telling me how relieved she was he'd arrived safely. She even brought a beautiful dark blue woolen blanket she had knitted. Our visit was pleasant and actually puzzled me. Had mother-hood given me a new perspective of Silja, or was she genuinely happy for us? I would never know.

Neighbors also visited, including my school friend, Nina, who I had not seen since our wedding. She had realized a short time ago that she was pregnant and consequently had many, many questions. I tried to answer all of them, realizing how misinformed a mother-to-be could become depending on her source of information. I did remind her that Mumo was a wonderful midwife, and later I saw them talking together.

While I spent each day caring for the baby and helping in the kitchen, Mumo and Ma both insisted that I rest in the afternoon, especially since I was up a couple of times each night to nurse. I relished those evening visits, my time to care for our baby by myself and to recognize that my milk was keeping him alive and thriving.

— —

Ma, with Abel's and my blessing, arranged for the christening. She had asked Pastor Ilikainen to come to our home, which made everything simpler. I was surprised he had agreed and appreciative at the same time. By then, Abel and I had decided to name our little boy Mikko. It wasn't a family name, but we liked that it meant "who is like God?" His name would remind us to teach him about his heavenly father and that we can never live up to the standards He wants for us. That's why He needed to send His Son to be our Savior.

Mikko was three weeks old when he was christened, and everything started out beautifully. Pastor Ilikainen used a Bible verse in the service, which he said we should help Mikko memorize as he grew older. It was John 3:16:

> For God so loved the world that He gave His only Son, that whoever be-
> lieves in Him should not perish, but have eternal life.

The pastor told us he would not be staying with us for dinner but asked if he could pray with us in private before he left. We stepped into Mumo's room, and he blessed us, asking for a safe journey to America, and that we would make a Christian home for Mikko and any other children with which we would be blessed.

Before he had even left the room I whispered to Abel, "How does he even know we'll be moving to America, and why would he want to pray with us now and not shortly before we leave?"

I heard Abel gasp as he held me and explained he had needed the pastor's help to process our traveling papers. "We have them, Eva, and we have passage. We'll be leaving from Kuopio on April third." That was less than two weeks away. I knew we would go, but it had never entered my mind it would be so soon.

"So when were you going to tell me this trivial news?" I asked as I squirmed out of his arms.

"Eva, this isn't like you. You knew we were going, and I just purchased our passage on Tuesday."

"Who else knows?" I asked, as tears ran down my cheeks.

"Pretty much everyone. The manifold is posted in the churches and in town."

I tried to gather my composure but finally asked Abel to leave me alone for a while. "I'll come back when I can." Up to that time I don't think I'd ever been so angry. I lay on the bed and wanted to kick my feet like a child, but instead I cried softly until I had no more tears.

Eventually Ma came in the room with a glass of wine and a wet washcloth. "Your guests are asking about you, Eva. Wash your face and drink this to settle your nerves. Abel didn't mean for you to be shocked. He thought we'd told you, and we thought he had, so you might as well be angry with us too." None of it made much sense to me, but I accepted her hug, washed my face, drank the wine, and felt a wee bit better.

Before we joined the guests I said, "It's really a farewell party, isn't it?"

"Yes, Eva, it is." With that reality confirmed, I joined my family and neighbors though from time to time I had to wipe my eyes. It wasn't terribly hard to explain: I was a new mother, and it had been an emotional day. "Forgive me," I said many times as I was hugged and the tears flowed anew. At a christening it is not unusual for the guests to give small gifts to the baby, but here people were also giving things for us to take to America.

My sisters gave me a beautiful skirt, shirt and apron, all embroidered with flowers and greens. It was a lavish gift, and as they hugged me, I realized they never expected to see me again. I wasn't ready to deal with that reality.

The eating and visiting went on for hours. I felt rescued when Mikko, who had been passed from guest to guest, needed to be nursed. As I sat in the rocking chair in Mumo's room, she came in as she often did, asking if this would be a good time for Abel to come in to talk with me. "He's worried about you."

"Not quite yet, Mumo. I don't mean to be such a baby."

"Don't give it another thought, little one. You said it yourself. You're a new mother, and it's been an emotional day."

Hearing my own words repeated I couldn't help but smile. "Yes, Mumo, but what am I going to do without you?"

"You are going to wake up to a new adventure every day, and you're going to pray to your Heavenly Father to make it a good day and a good life. Don't ever forget you're a Finn, and that you have Sisu. Think of how well you went through your pregnancy and birthing. Abel and Mikko are very blessed to have you as a wife and mother."

"Mumo, what will I do when our next baby is ready to be born?"

"You will read everything you've written down in your notebooks about birthing, and then you'll either find a midwife or you'll deliver your baby yourself. Besides your body will remember."

I gasped. "That doesn't sound good at all. Do you know how much I'll miss you?"

"If it's as much as I'll miss you, I do. But now I'll go get Abel before he thinks you've run away."

I nodded my agreement and barely let him come in before I told him how sorry I was for being so upset. He apologized, which meant a lot to me, for shocking me, and then he kissed Mikko and me and led the way back to the party. Tears were never far away as I thanked everyone for coming, for their gifts, and accepted their farewells. As the house emptied and even Abel left with his family, Ma gave me the wonderful news that my sisters and their families wouldn't be leaving until the next day.

We cleaned up food and dishes, put out bread, cheese, sausage, and fruit for anyone who might need a snack before the day was over and chatted like three school girls. Mumo had the grand idea of having my two nieces and nephew bunk with her. She said she'd take care of them. Ma made makeshift beds for the sons-in-law in the kitchen and did the same for her three daughters and Mikko in the parlor. It was a wonderful plan, allowing us to have the whole evening to reminisce. I loved my sisters and knew I would miss them.

Marta said I'd be so busy having babies I wouldn't have time to miss them, but I knew she was wrong. We made solemn vows to write to each other and to pray for each other's family.

Ilona dug and dug until I told her why I'd been so upset earlier, and when I explained about the shock that we were leaving so soon, she responded, "What a relief to know Abel isn't perfect." We laughed and laughed at that remark and then discussed differences between men and women. Marta and Ilona felt they both had good marriages and were glad to see I did too, but they were also quick to admit that marriage wasn't always easy. The conversation went on and on as only sisters can talk. Finally our eyes grew heavy and we gave in to sleep. Though I woke twice during the night to tend to Mikko, we all slept in, only getting up when we were no longer able to ignore the aroma of fresh coffee. True to her word, Mumo took care of the children, who seemed delighted with themselves.

What a gift we'd been given we all agreed as we made preparations for their departure. When they all left, amid tears and hugs, the house seemed way too quiet, and I realized I was emotionally worn out. After nursing Mikko, I handed him off to an ever willing Mumo and slept the afternoon away.

8

Preparations

"For I know the thoughts that I think toward you, saith the LORD, thoughts of peace, and not of evil, to give you an expected end."

JEREMIAH 29:11

In less than two weeks we would be leaving, but for me there was little to do. Abel had already taken most of my belongings and packed them in our trunk. I sorted through the gifts we'd received, and knowing our trunk space was limited, designated only a few items to go with us. The rest I packed in a box, which Pa promised to mail once we had a permanent address.

Ma came up with a wonderful idea of sewing pockets onto my travel skirt and coat. In these I placed necessities such as soap, handkerchiefs, and a hairbrush and an oilcloth envelope in which to put nappies. Mumo put a notebook and a pencil in one pocket, saying I'd probably have plenty of time to write while we traveled. She once again told me to "keep writing so I would understand."

When Abel arrived on Tuesday he was impressed with the travel pockets and asked me to sew some on his traveling coat also. He especially wanted to have some safe place to put our tickets, money, key to our trunk and traveling papers. He brought a vest and his coat the next morning, obviously eager to have the alterations made, so he could fill the pockets. While we had coffee, he explained to all of us how we would sail to London from Kuopio and from there to a town in Canada called Toronto. Once we got there we had railroad passes to take us to Cloquet, Minnesota, which was in the United States. We'd make a homestead claim there for land to its east in an area named Esko, which supposedly had many Finnish settlers. He surprised me with all he knew. He'd even been given the name of a family to contact in Cloquet that would be willing to help us get settled.

Some families took years before they settled down, but Abel seemed determined to get his farm started right away. He explained he wanted to get crops in this spring. He said he would build a small barn first and then a sauna, and that he'd also make a small cottage to keep us through the winter. His eyes sparkled as he talked about "our farm". To my surprise I was catching his excitement.

On April third Abel's entire family came to Ma's and Pa's in two wagons right after milking. I had expected Eero to drive us the 30 miles to Kuopio, but instead it would be Arvo and Margit since two cows were due to calf any time. I looked at the large, wooden trunk in the wagon, wondering how we'd even be able to lift it. I loaded a small bundle, containing nappies, fresh clothing for Mikko, cheese, dry fruit, sausage, and rye crackers.

We hugged good-bye, knowing we would never see each other again, and, when the pain became too great to bear, I climbed on the wagon, leaning against the trunk. Abel handed Mikko to me and climbed up beside us. Arvo started off, and we were on our way. I took one last look at the pleasant little farm and my loving family and recognized once again how blessed I'd been. Abel must have realized tears were on the way because as he put his arm around me, he whispered, "Sisu, Eva. We're going to have a good life."

Three hours later we were at the docks in Kuopio, happy to get down from the wagon. Abel immediately spotted the Astraea, the steamship that would take us to London. He and Arvo carried the trunk aboard while Margit and I looked around at the milling people. When the men returned, they told us it would be three hours until the ship left, and said they would find some lunch for us. They returned with a brown bag containing freshly fried fish, bread, and cider for all of us. Sitting by the sea, the food tasted wonderful. We had never felt very close to Arvo and Margit, but they were friendly and kind. They surprised us by saying they planned to go to America as soon as they could scrape together enough money for passage. Abel told them he would send our address home as soon as we were settled, but if they didn't get it, they should go to Esko and track us down. Arvo said he was done with farming, so thought they'd go to Michigan, and he'd look for work in the copper mines. Margit held Mikko while we talked, confiding that she didn't think they'd have any children. Her eyes looked so sad, and I felt sorry for not reaching out to her.

The horses ate their oats and drank water while we ate, and when everyone's stomach was full, we thanked and hugged Margit and Arvo, wishing each other well. They walked with us to the ship where Abel presented our papers and tickets, which were examined and stamped, and we were allowed to board. We waved good-bye to Arvo and Margit as they walked toward the wagon. I wondered whether they would really come to America and whether we'd see them there. I wondered also whether or not they'd have children and said a silent prayer that they would.

Abel led me to our steerage quarters, which was really the cargo hold of the ship. Cargo was on both ends, but in the middle were wide numbered benches. I spotted our trunk with relief, and we went to sit by it. I was glad to see it remained locked since it contained everything we owned.

Someone was yelling above for all passengers to come aboard. In a short time the benches filled and the ship pulled away from the pier. I had never been on a ship before but enjoyed the rocking motion. Mikko must have liked it also as he fell asleep right away. Abel said he wanted to stretch his legs, but I was content to stretch out on the bench and watch Mikko sleep. I spotted water barrels at the ends of the benches and curtained off areas where we could relieve ourselves. There was a pleasant humming as I heard people all around me speaking in Finn. It amazed me that of the 100 or so people I could see, I didn't know one.

9

We Sail

"I can do all things through Christ that strengthenth me."

PHILIPPIANS 4:13

The trip to London was monotonous but comfortable. I speculated that all of the passengers were tired from preparations. The men mostly stayed on deck while the women and children were below in the steerage section. I talked a bit with a young mother with three little ones, but she fretted so much about her children's safety that I took Mikko back to our spot to enjoy being with him.

Sleeping on the benches was not difficult. The movement of the ship was soothing and relaxing. When I awoke the second morning I heard a man with a megaphone making announcements first in English, then in Finnish and finally in Swedish: "Prepare to land in 90 minutes. Nothing you leave behind can be reclaimed. The crew will assist with trunks if needed." We had taken little out so there was little to repack. I had rinsed Mikko's diapers, wrapped them in oilcloth, and tucked them in one of my coat pockets. I'd wash and dry them when we boarded the Sinclair. I was sure there would be more room. Abel had told me we would receive two meals each day, so I supposed we'd have a dining room.

The departure from the ship went smoothly. Abel said he wanted to find the Sinclair and get our trunk loaded right away though the ship was not scheduled to leave until late afternoon. I walked beside him, trying to match his long strides as he followed the wagon that held our trunk along with hundreds of others.

We walked at least a mile along the piers before Abel stopped before a huge ship. It looked like a small city to me rising high above the water. Abel checked in with a man standing at the bottom of the steps and was told we could board at any time but once aboard we couldn't leave the ship. We were both eager to see where we would be spending the next two weeks. The man checked our paperwork, took our tickets, and checked off our names in a large notebook. He also asked our final destination, and Abel proudly answered Esko, Minnesota, United States of America. The man smiled and said we could board. Abel asked about out trunk, and the man pointed to a dray stacked with trunks. We found ours, and the man whistled to crew members to load it after he had marked it with the number 204. The trunk was carried up the steep steps, and we followed right behind it. The trunk went on its way, but we were stopped at the top, and once again our paperwork was checked. This time it was quickly done and the man yelled out, "Assistance to steerage 204 and 205."

The smallest man I had ever seen led us down flights of stairs until we came to a large room. Once again, cargo was at both ends, but this time metal bunks were lined up between. Black numbers were painted on the beds, and we soon found 204 and 205. We were relieved to see our trunk right by our bunks. Abel said he would take the top, so there was no danger of Mikko falling so far, and I appreciated that offer. After getting somewhat settled, which meant spreading out our coats and washing diapers in a tub of water meant exactly for that purpose, I nursed Mikko, while Abel ate the last of our bread and I ate an apple, and then we went back up on the deck to be in the fresh air and to watch passengers board.

I asked Abel how many people he thought would be on the ship, and he told me about a thousand passengers and a crew of a hundred. That seemed to be an unbelievable number, but as I watched the people board I knew he must be right. As it grew closer to the departure time, the pace of people loading grew faster, and everywhere we saw people laughing and crying. One little boy, about three, was obviously separated from his parents and was wailing in fear. I was relieved to see a crew member pick him up and return him to his mother. I saw a finely dressed lady drop her bag as she was boarding and couldn't be comforted as she saw her belongings float and then sink into the unforgiving water. Abel kept his arm around Mikko and me for which I was thankful. We stayed on deck until tugboats pushed our ship away from the pier.

When Mikko called our attention to his hunger, we made the return trip to steerage, which was now, crowded, noisy, and smelly. This would be our home for the next two weeks, so I knew I had to make the best of it.

Later that afternoon, my misconceptions about dining were disproved. Four pairs of men (I think they were called stewards) came down the stairs carrying huge pots. Each pair started at one end of a row and ladled watery soup into metal bowls hanging with a spoon at the end of our bunk bed. They cursed our large trunk as they scooted over it. Shortly after, teen-age boys went through the aisles tossing bread to each passenger. They pointed to barrels where we could rinse our dishes and others where we could get drinking water. The soup and bread were very ordinary, but they filled our stomachs. Abel and I took turns using the toilets, so one of us could stay with Mikko and also watch our belongings. Abel told me he didn't completely trust the people on the ship, and I had to admit many looked desperate. We probably looked that way too.

The seventeen days on the ship were tedious and humbling. I had never thought much about the differences in the lives of the rich and the poor. In fact, I had never considered myself poor, but as I compared the treatment of the steerage passengers to others, I was shocked. We were given a bed for a temporary home, fed poor quality food, and not allowed to show ourselves on deck except for a short time each day and then in restricted areas. Occasionally, during trips to and from the deck, we'd glimpse other passengers—many in finery, enjoying themselves. It was an interesting discovery. When I talked with Abel about it, he barely reacted, saying there had always been differences between rich and poor and always would be. He said I'd been sheltered by being raised in a loving family and always having a nice home and good food. He did tell me that America would be a land of opportunity. I was ready to get there. In the meantime I had an opportunity to start writing in one of the journals Mumo had given me. I wasn't sure where to start my story, so I started to write many of the Bible verses Mumo had helped me learn as a child. Before long I knew exactly when our story had begun.

10

Entry

"Cast thy burden upon the LORD, and He shall sustain thee......"

PSALMS 55:22

The ship came to shore early in the afternoon before we'd even been given our meager servings of soup and bread. The hustle and bustle in steerage confirmed everyone's eagerness to leave the ship. As the days had gone by, the close quarters and human smells had become disgusting, and a diet of porridge for breakfast and soup for supper along with stale bread became very old. Our plans to leave immediately came to an end when we learned that our stairway was blocked. One young man somehow made it through the blockade only to return shortly telling us to "stay put" because steerage passengers would be the last to leave the ship. That policy worked to our advantage since while we were waiting Abel recruited a young man to help with our trunk.

We were finally allowed to leave, and once again Abel wanted to find our train immediately, knowing that a train to Minnesota left each afternoon. Instead of being allowed to find our train, we were herded into a large building where we were inspected by health officials and asked many questions. Worst of all, Mikko and I were separated from Abel who was sent to a line for men only. At the last moment, he gave me papers for Mikko and myself, and the examination of them was the first step in a line that moved unbearably slowly. Following that, we were told to completely undress and to tie a numbered card to the bundle we made of our clothes. The same number on a string was handed to us to put around our necks. The humility of standing naked amongst strangers was bad enough, but Mikko, who was obviously cold, started to cry loudly. He continued crying inconsolably while we were led to a shower. There must have been 20 women with children packed in a shower room at a time. I had never seen a shower before but enjoyed the luxury of cleansing myself, especially after a kind woman offered to hold Mikko, so I was able to wash myself, even my hair. When she handed him back, I realized how plump and healthy he looked. With the steaminess of the shower, he was warm again, so no longer crying, but then we suffered the indignity of being sprayed with an awful smelling spray and being handed back our clothing which was damp with the same spray. I later learned that everyone and everything in steerage was sprayed with some kind of a disinfectant to prevent vermin from entering Canada.

We weren't allowed to dress until we were examined by women who did not speak Finnish and were none too gentle. Worst of all they had the responsibility to decide whether we were fit to enter their country. Mikko and I were healthy and were passed through quickly. We were allowed to dress as we stood in line for an eye exam that was horrible. Poor Mikko screamed as a doctor looked under his eyelids. I didn't scream, but my eyes teared greatly as the doctor rolled my eyelids over some kind of a stick. I was very relieved when he stamped our papers and our number cards, and directed me to follow the line to the right. I couldn't help noticing that a line to the left was moving slowly and that each person had another card around their neck with a bold letter (I remember seeing E, B and T), which must have indicated a disease or weakness. Though

I felt pity for those people, I left the area as quickly as possible, wanting to get away from my own humiliation and the sorrow of others. What would I do if the next time I saw Abel, he had a letter on him? With that awful thought in my mind I searched the sea of people frantically until I spotted his head high above most of the other men. I joined the pushing and shoving until I reached him only to find him talking happily with Johann, the young man who had helped him with our trunk. He paused long enough to nod at me and express his need to find some food and space. He, Johann, and the trunk cleared a path which I gladly followed, holding Mikko tightly to me.

With bowls of stew, purchased from a food stand, in our stomachs, we walked until we found a sign for the railroad for which we had tickets. I was surprised to see Johann still with us, and even more surprised when Abel announced he was buying a ticket for him to go with us to Cloquet. I looked at him with puzzlement, but then Abel said if it was all right with me, he'd like Johann to work for us the first year, so we could not only get fields planted but get a cottage, sauna, and barn built more quickly. There was no way I would object with those goals in mind. The thought of being settled in a cottage of our own sounded too good to be true. I had no idea how Abel expected to pay Johann but put up no objection, knowing it would be useless anyway.

By showing our rail tickets to people who appeared friendly, we were led not to the train station but to a trolley that took the four of us and our trunk to the train depot. Without being able to speak English, showing our tickets worked like magic. The rail workers guided us to the train, gesturing that it would be leaving soon. Abel checked us in as we rejoiced over the wonderful timing, knowing people sometimes waited days at the train station.

As we boarded the train I felt we would be traveling in luxury for the next few days. We had two large seats that faced each other, and our trunk was put in the baggage car. Someone had painted our name and Esko, Minnesota, USA on it, so we no longer felt we were in danger of losing it.

I didn't see any other Finns aboard, but I did meet a Swedish family who knew enough Finnish to visit, which I knew would make the trip go faster. They planned to settle in the iron mining towns north of Cloquet. They gave us their names and the name of the town where they planned to settle, and we did the same. The family was so congenial that I felt we had our first friends in America. Their nine-year-old daughter, Annika, was especially fascinated by Mikko and offered to take care of him while I attempted to tame my wild hair. After finding my brush, I was delighted to tend to it, returning to the usual braid I wore. I asked my new friend if she thought there was a way to wash diapers, and before I knew it, she had managed to get two pails of hot water from an attendant. I moved to the back of the car, which was empty, and used the bar of soap I had brought from home. When I had unpacked the diapers from the oilcloth I had wrapped them in, I had to turn my head away from the stench of ammonia. I scrubbed and scrubbed and happily rinsed them in the other pail of water. I even washed out the oilcloth. Nothing was perfect, but everything was so much better. The attendant took the used water away, and as if reading my mind, he showed me where I could hang the diapers between the two cars. I dropped one, which flew into the countryside, but held on to the others, which dried quickly. As I took them down, I realized how much I had taken conveniences, such as a clothesline, for granted.

Returning to our seats, I saw Abel and Johann huddled over our empty lunch bag. "Eva, what do you think?" Abel asked. As I looked closer, I saw they were sketching the plans for a cottage, our cottage. "Anything you'd like to change?"

"Since Johann will be living with us, and probably will marry, how about adding a room to the other end?" I noticed Johann blushing as well as nodding enthusiastically. Abel penciled in another room and then asked about shelves for the kitchen. Johann piped up, "It's easy to add shelves and maybe some bins too—if you want them." As details were added to the drawing, I grew increasingly excited. A home of our own sounded wonderful. I knew Abel would be able to build a cottage but that the fields would tend to be his priority. As I talked to Johann, I learned that he had been an apprentice to his carpenter father and was eager to try his skills, wanting eventually to start his own carpentry business. It appeared that he and Abel would work well together. Just as Mikko was waking up hungry, we decided we should have shelves on most walls and not the bins, so we could keep our supplies away from varmints and even away from Mikko as he grew into a toddler.

On the back of the cottage plan, Abel started a list of the things we would need right away for the farm. We brainstormed until the list grew long:

draft horse
wagon
bridles and reins
anvil
stove
wash tubs
pails
2 cows
12 chickens
2 lambs
2 pigs
seed potatoes
seeds
flour
cornmeal
sugar
coffee
yeast
leavening

oatmeal
potatoes
carrots
onions
rutabagas
salt pork
lard
kerosene lamps (3)
kerosene

"You are a rich man if you're able to buy all of that," Johann said with respect.

"It will take almost all of our savings, but it should work out," Abel said.

"You better add salt and pepper and feed for the animals, and matches," I said. With those additions he put the list in his pocket, and we all relaxed, feeling prepared for the next step in our adventure. Being on land, even if we were on a train, was encouraging. Before night fell, we bought one more meal of stew, bread and weak coffee and packed up our belongings. We woke to the attendant announcing we were in Minnesota.

11

A New Beginning

"The eternal God is thy refuge and underneath are the everlasting arms...."

DEUTERONOMY 33:27

The train's first stop in Minnesota was International Falls, then Hibbing where we said sad farewells to our newly made friends. Little Annika was teary-eyed as she said good-bye to Mikko, who made matters worse as he smiled so big it looked like he was trying to turn himself inside out. The next stop was Duluth which is right next to Lake Superior, and then we were on to Cloquet. The trip there was short and mostly uphill.

As our stop was made, we eagerly left the train, claimed our precious trunk from the baggage car, and tried to find our bearings. Our big advantage was that it was a Finnish community, so when Abel asked for the general store, we were pointed in the right direction. We were told the store was about a mile away, but after walking a half mile our stomachs were grumbling, and we stopped at a food stand to buy pasties, a delicious meat pie we had never eaten before.

With stomachs full the rest of the walk went easily. Our eyes were big as we walked along the wooden sidewalks. I had never seen so much wood. There were huge stacks of lumber, logs floated in the river that meandered alongside the town. The buildings were all made of wood also. As we walked, people stopped us asking where we were from. They'd introduce themselves and admire Mikko. We were talking with so many people that we almost missed the General Store, which would have been embarrassing since it took up almost a whole block. Johann and I sat on the trunk while Abel went in to meet Mr. Wirtanen. Within minutes his wife, a stocky woman who never stopped smiling, invited us in, telling Johann to leave the trunk right where it was. We walked through the store, which was crowded with a huge assortment of food, tools, equipment, furniture, hardware, stacks and stacks of lumber, and even baby chicks.

The Wirtanens lived in the back in two crowded, but neat rooms. Mrs. Wirtanen invited us to sit down as she poured coffee and served buns. Her husband called for her almost as soon as she'd sat down, and she laughingly excused herself, saying, "The customer always comes first." Before she returned, three school age children came in the back door, threw down their books, grabbed buns, and went back outside. Abel and Mr. Wirtanen soon came in saying they were going to the land office, but we should stay put. Within an hour they returned with Abel holding papers and looking as proud as I'd ever seen him. "We are now officially homesteaders," he said, and Mr. Wirtanen shook everyone's hand saying we'd gotten a beautiful piece of land. He explained it had been forfeited only a few days ago since the young man who had claimed it got too lonely and moved back to the rest of his family, who were living in Duluth. He said he'd made sure that the land office hadn't announced it was available since he knew we'd be coming soon.

"How will I ever thank you? Abel asked Mr. Wirtanen.

"Just continue to be a good customer," was his immediate reply, "and tell newcomers about me."

Mr. Wirtanen and Abel went back to the store, and Mrs. Wirtanen returned to start supper. "You're going to stay here tonight, and Arvid will take you to your place in the morning. It's Saturday tomorrow, so Arvid, Jr. will help me mind the store. Now tell me about your trip, and let me hold that beautiful baby."

The evening was wonderful. Arvid and Agnes were full of fun and in love with life. Their store was successful, due to the many settlers and the families moving in to work in the lumber industry. He was optimistic that the business would grow even more and said his next plan was to start a smaller establishment in Esko, so people wouldn't have to go so far to buy their supplies.

— —

The next morning, after sleeping on floor mattresses, we left with their wagon loaded down with our trunk, a stove, an anvil, tubs and pails, food supplies, baby chicks and bales of hay. Arvid and Abel talked continually as we headed to our new land. He told Abel that he could get the livestock right in Esko. In fact, he'd go with Abel to get some before he returned to Cloquet.

We traveled on what Arvid Wirtanen called a corduroy road because it was covered with logs to keep it passable during muddy springs and heavy rains. The road wound through wooded areas. Occasionally we'd see farms, but for the most part the land was not cleared.

I spotted a sign, ESKO, and had my first glimpse of the community in which we'd live. I spotted a mill, a store, a school, and a church before we turned a corner. In a short time, Mr. Wirtanen announced we'd arrived at our land. He stopped the wagon near a large stand of tall pines.

Johann whistled at the trees, saying "Will you look at all that lumber just waiting to be made into cottages, fences and such!"

Abel went right to the open fields feeling and smelling the soil with obvious satisfaction. Abel and Johann unloaded the wagon while Arvid showed me around, pointing out that we had "40 mighty fine acres that included fine lumber, already cleared fields, a lean-to, and access to a river." He told me there was a well somewhere too. Soon he whistled to Abel and told him they'd better go back to Esko to get livestock so he could get back to work. Abel and he hurriedly left with the wagon.

Johann assembled the stove while I gathered wood to fuel it. While I was looking for wood, I found a deserted chair, a few rusty tools, wooden crates, and pots and pans. The best finds, however, were a large spool of rope, which we could put to use for tethering animals and for a clothes-line and the pump which brought us sweet water from our well.

Abel and Arvid came back much sooner than we expected with a strong horse, two cows, two pigs, two lambs and three grown hens, so we would have eggs soon.

Arvid took his horse but said he would leave the wagon until next week when he'd pick it up. "You'll need shelter, and sleeping on the wagon will be much warmer than on the ground." We all shook his hand, thanking him for his help. As he was leaving he told us Agnes had sent with lunch which we'd find on the wagon. He took off on his horse, obviously in a hurry to return to his store.

We found Agnes' basket filled with sandwiches, cookies, raisins, and lemonade and ate our fill, using the trunk as a table. The men decided the first thing they needed to do was make pens for the livestock. Johann convinced Abel to cut down their first pine trees, which he would use to make a split rail fence. Abel had intended to use the lean-to, but Johann explained to him how he would be able to easily convert it into a temporary barn for milking. I enjoyed seeing the two of them discussing what they would do and coming to shared decisions.

With lunch done and appreciated and with Mikko fed and sleeping on the wagon, I started unpacking our trunk in earnest and planning the evening meal. Once I'd found a knife and a pot, I started chopping potatoes, onions, carrots and salt pork. I realized I needed to remind the men to start hunting or we'd get very tired of salt pork. Nonetheless I put everything in my pot, covered it with the water, so it would be ready to cook later and then mixed flour, yeast, salt and water for a couple of loaves of whole wheat bread. I purposely made a small batch in case the new oven was finicky. As soon as the dough was set aside to rise, I started a fire in the stove, feeding it carefully. Before I knew it Mikko was awake and needing a change of nappies and of location. I was learning to do as much as I could while he slept, so I could be available for him when he was awake. I carried him over to the livestock, which were grazing in the field as they were tethered to trees. The cows were very contented, and I looked forward to milking them that evening. The pigs were busy grubbing in the dirt. I felt sorry for the horse, who didn't have horse company, but she didn't seem to mind. It was the lambs that fascinated Mikko. They scampered as far as their tether would allow and then went in the opposite direction. The baas, moos, oinks and neighs were music to my farm girl ears. The animals' sweet temperaments would make life easier for all of us.

I set Mikko under a birch tree on his blanket, and he cooed as the tree branches moved above him. There were tight leaf buds, but none were open yet. While he watched the tree, I put our soup onto cook, fired the stove one more time, formed the dough into loaves, put them in the warming drawer, and covered them to rise. While I was tending the stove, Johann and Abel came to retrieve the animals. They took the cows, lambs and pigs to their new pens which looked sturdy. Abel filled their water pails also, again exclaiming how sweet the water was. When I put the bread in the oven and the soup was bubbling away, I knew it had been a good, productive day.

We ate our simple but satisfying supper, and I cleaned up the few dishes we'd used. Abel suggested I keep the fire in the stove going and that he and Johann would move the wagon close to it. With that done we all decided to tour our farm one more time. The farm was bordered by roads on two sides, the river on one, and the beautiful pine forest on the other.

We started at the forest, enjoying the scent of pine and the soft needles on the ground. What a fun place for Mikko to play as he grew up. As we entered deeper, the woods filled with shadows, and we all spotted rabbits and even deer. "This is a real treasure," Johann whispered. "What a great place! You'll have lumber and fuel for the next 50 years and meat for your table."

Abel led us to the fields, pointing out areas that had been plowed and others that looked as if they'd never been touched by man. He'd scoop up soil in his hand and smell it. "That is good quality," he said many times.

When we got to the river, I knew I'd found my favorite place. Johann must have noticed my eagerness to explore and offered to hold Mikko. I agreed and walked down to the river which had birch and poplar growing on both sides. The river water was icy cold, and I spotted a few fish, more deer, and a perfect picnic spot.

The sun began to set, and our walk came to an end just as Johann discovered red osier growing, which he said would be great to use for making baskets.

Our world seemed full of possibilities. Johann handed Mikko to Abel, to my surprise, and ran ahead of us to the pines. By the time we arrived at the wagon, he had begun covering it with pine boughs to make a softer bed. I put a blanket down to cover them and was impressed how good it felt and smelled. Mikko was the first to try it out, and after feeding the stove, making sure our belongings were somewhat protected, and removing our foot wear we joined him. Abel and I shared a quilt, so we could have the benefit of each other's warmth and Johann used another.

Our sleeping conditions were all the better as I looked up into the sky and began to recognize constellations. I started to tell the men that in Finland we could see the same stars, but they were sound asleep already. I started to pray, but that first night, as well as many others, I'm afraid I fell asleep in the middle of doing so.

12

Plans

"But my God shall supply all your needs according to His riches in glory by
Jesus Christ."

PHILIPPIANS 4:19

The next morning as I sat on the wagon nursing Mikko, we all began talking of what we each needed to do before Mr. Wirtanen returned for his wagon. Abel was insistent that he get potatoes and other cold weather crops in the ground by May first, which was only a little over a week away, so he said his emphasis was on plowing and planting. He felt that once the early crops were in, both he and Johann could build the cottage.

Johann seemed concerned that we'd be caught in cold weather and/or rain. Since our first night on the farm was none too warm, he wanted to start building right away. As Abel looked at Mikko and me, he seemed to realize the need for shelter, and in the end, they decided to do work on their own priorities that day, work together on fields on Monday, and on the cottage on Tuesday. They asked if I could finish unpacking on my own, and I said of course, but I also needed to do laundry and keep us in food. Abel told me as soon as I found his rifle, I should set it aside, so he could shoot some rabbits.

I unpacked all day Sunday, sorting things into the wooden crates we'd found. I was amazed at how much had been packed in the large trunk and realized anew why the trunk was so precious to Abel. I put the crates of things we wouldn't want to get wet under the wagon along with the crate of baby chicks. I was concerned by the small amount of food we had and our big appetites, so was relieved when Abel shot three rabbits that evening. Though not a fan of rabbit, the aroma of them cooking the next day as I made more bread and hard tack to supplement stews and soups, was wonderful. The cows had adjusted well enough to their new home, and I enjoyed milking them. We stored the milk in jars in the river, and it kept very well chilled.

Besides Abel's rifle, he was thrilled when I unpacked the plow that he would use on the fields. I was surprised the plow had fit, but Abel and his father had taken it apart to make the best use of room. Abel pushed it through the earth, and though I could see it took all of his strength to use, he seemed very pleased when one whole field was plowed to his satisfaction.

Before the day was over, we had our first visitors, Esa and Lempi Raisanen along with two of their children, six-year-old Jussi and ten-year-old Otto. They introduced themselves, pointed out the direction of their house and treated us to coffee and cake they had brought with them. Within minutes we felt as if we had known them for years. They admired Mikko and our land and then said they needed to go home but wondered if they could bring us to church on Sunday. When we agreed, they said they'd pick us up at nine and were on their way.

True to their word, the men both worked on the cabin on Tuesday, erecting two walls from the pine trees Johann had cut down and split.

Abel surprised me by saying he'd like to keep working on the cottage until the outer walls were up. Each night there had been heavy frost, and he was realizing his goal for planting was too early. We'd also lost almost half of our baby chicks to a very sneaky fox, so getting them inside was a high priority.

That first week was a blur of activities. By Friday afternoon, the men had built an outhouse, a small coop for chickens, and all of the outer walls of the cottage had been erected. They had made a temporary roof from pine boughs, but Johann was working on pine shingles. The men would not cut windows in the walls until they had purchased glass, and the door just leaned against its opening, needing hinges, but we had a safe shelter in which to sleep. They moved the trunk, the stove and the crates of our things inside, and I had the joy of arranging our supplies in a more permanent home. As if our timing had been ordained by God, that afternoon rain started and lasted for the next few days. Our cottage stayed surprisingly dry, and the men were very industrious during the rain, and with the exception of caring for the animals, they began building furniture: a table and two chairs, two beds, and a cradle for Mikko. It began to look very homey inside, and although the furniture was in Johann's words "crude at best", I loved it.

Our three kerosene lamps were not enough to light the entire cottage but added some cheer. Besides, by dark we were all bone tired. Abel drew in windows with chalk, and Johann disappeared for a while, returning with several pegs he'd whittled for hooks in the bedrooms and kitchen. I told him I'd like at least a dozen more, when he had time, and shelves to keep our things off the floor.

Having gathered our first two eggs, I made pancakes and salt pork for supper along with a jar of cloud berry preserves Mumo had sent with us and strong coffee. It was our first meal prepared and eaten in our cottage, and we all felt pleased and nourished with the results.

13

A Church Family

"...for this day is holy unto our Lord: neither be ye sorry; for the joy of the LORD is your strength.

NEHEMIAH 8:10

On Saturday morning, just as he'd promised, Arvid Wirtanen arrived on his horse, ready to retrieve his wagon. It was the first day of sunshine in four days, and I was busy washing clothes. Even with the door open, the cabin was humid, but that didn't deter me. I was relieved to finally be able to boil nappies and hang them outside to be bleached by the sun. Abel and Johann showed him the cottage, and I heard him admire the progress we'd made. I also heard him encourage Abel to return to his store to purchase windows and to replace the "country" furniture with some of his merchandise. He was a natural salesman, and we enjoyed our time with him even if Johann and Abel's faces turned red when he spoke of replacing the furniture. Once again he left a parcel from Agnes, which contained bread, butter, and cookies. Bless that woman! He also left a box of nails, which he said was his gift to us. He left with his wagon 30 minutes after he'd arrived, telling us he had many wagons for sale at his store.

After finishing my stacks of laundry, I realized how dirty we all were and was determined to bathe that evening. After supper and clean up, Abel carried pails of heated water outside close to the river, while I carried Mikko, a blanket and clean clothes for all of us. Peeling off layer after layer of grime, I promised myself never to get so dirty again. I put our stinky clothing into a gunny sack I'd brought for that purpose, and we began to scrub ourselves using scrub brushes and soap. Abel and I could even scrub each other's back, a ritual usually left for the sauna. We quickly dipped into the icy water, and though we couldn't stay in long, we felt squeaky clean. After putting on a warm nightgown, I washed Mikko in one of the tubs. The bath was a new experience, and he laughed as the soap bubbles he touched broke. I wrapped a blanket around Mikko and myself, and we returned to the cabin while Abel nested the pails and tubs and carried them and the bag of dirty clothes back also. As I walked I noticed the start of a path from the river to our cottage. I also saw ferns and Mayflowers poking up out of the soil. Spring was on its way!

Johann went to the river next, carrying his hot water. He had told us recently more about his girl in Finland. I wondered if he thought of her when he saw Abel and me together. While Johann was gone, Abel brushed out my hair, and I trimmed his hair and beard. We only had a small hand mirror, but we both felt more civilized.

Esa, Lempi and their children arrived right at 9 the next morning. We were all set in our good clothes, and though they were wrinkled, we felt much more respectable. To our surprise Johann had told us he was not a believer and that he would stay home, doing some more whittling.

The ride to the Finnish Apostolic Church was surprisingly short. The little wooden church, painted white, had a cross on top of it and was very beautiful. Before sitting down in a pew, Esa and Lempi introduced us to the 30 or so people attending, including a lay pastor. The service, conducted in Finnish, was wonderful. For a while as I listened to the music and Finnish words, I felt we were back in Finland. There, however, the church was very large and much further away from home, making weekly attendance rare. After church, we all enjoyed coffee and pulla, so light it melted on our tongues. We enjoyed visiting, and knew without a doubt, we'd be here often. I treasured the family names I heard (Mattinens, Kinnunens, Sunnarborgs, Juntunens, Liupakkas, to name a few). They were music to my ears.

We were happy to be able to answer the lay pastor's questions about our baptisms and confirmation. When we told him where we lived, he said he'd make a visit the coming week.

Abel, in the meantime, found many farmers to talk with, seeking information about the growing season. The women admired little Mikko, who slept angelically. For a while I didn't even know where he was, but was happily reunited when he started to cry.

As Esa drove us back home, he answered questions about the people we'd met. Though I could remember few names, we felt we were in the process of making new friends with many people. Esa followed a different way home, showing us the Esko School, a small grocery store, the creamery, and a small lumber yard. Esa told us the Esko lumber yard prices were far less than at Wirtanens, and you could even get a little credit "without paying an arm and a leg." I had to ask Abel what he had meant by that, but didn't get an answer until I asked Johann. I continually made good and bad discoveries.

While we'd been gone, Johann had been busy with his knife and plane, this time making blocks and the start of a train for Mikko, who chewed on them all, letting us know teeth were on the way.

14

Work & Its Rewards

"...If God be for us, who can be against us?"

ROMANS 8:31

The days and weeks of that first spring and summer went quickly and happily. Just as they had worked together on the cabin, Abel and Johann worked in the fields, planting potatoes, onions, corn, swedes (rutabagas) ,wheat, oats, and rye. I had my little kitchen garden close to our cottage, and it was filled with lettuce, spinach, beans, peas, beets, tomatoes, parsley, dill, and cucumbers, as well as flowers. Abel had opened more ground. We all removed the many rocks we found making a large pile near the river. Johann didn't tell us what he was planning but asked us to save the rocks for the sauna.

Johann continued making improvements on our cottage, installing windows, putting hinges on the doors, installing shelves and even a few drawers. He sealed the roof and continued making furniture, toys and implements. He was especially fond of whittling in the evening while I knitted or mended. Abel enjoyed spending that time with Mikko, reading or playing with him. Mikko entertained us all with his happy-go-lucky personality. He was ever so interested in the world and would sit happily watching birds or bugs while I did endless weeding. He babbled constantly and when he pointed to something he expected me to tell him its name. By the beginning of summer he was easily sitting by himself and by the end of summer he was crawling everywhere. Abel pointed out one evening that we badly needed a wooden floor and rug for Mikko to crawl on, but we both knew our savings was down to less than a dollar, so they, along with many other items would have to wait.

Johann made a wagon for us with high sides. For the first time Abel made an exception to his own rule and used credit to buy four wooden wheels and the two axles needed. I knew credit made Abel very uncomfortable, but he said we absolutely needed a wagon to go to market to sell our produce.

In mid-August we loaded our wagon with vegetables: potatoes, onions, carrots and corn. Abel had learned about open markets in West Duluth and looked forward to selling our crops. It would be our first income since coming to America. He asked me to come with him, saying we should be back by the early afternoon. I was happy to go with and asked if I could take some of my garden with also. Abel had no objection to my doing so, and I added lettuce, beets, cucumbers, beans and peas as well as a variety of my flowers to the wagon and even a dozen jars of jam I'd made from the abundant supply of wild berries.

The ride to West Duluth didn't take much more than an hour, and Abel seemed to know right where to go on Grand Avenue. I looked at other cartloads and wagons of goods and knew Abel's produce was just as good if not better. I had fun displaying his produce as he made signs of cardboard, marking prices. He did not know how to write their names in English, but he referred to his goods in their English names. He had a good ear for language, while I found English very confusing.

I noticed right away that while men would go to any of the displays, women seemed to be attracted to our wagon. I believe they liked seeing another woman and a child. To Abel's surprise my bouquets, tied with string bows, were the first things to sell. Abel enjoyed talking with the customers while I could only listen, nod, or say a few words. A few Finns stopped, and I enjoyed talking with them. The morning went fast, as the entire wagon was emptied, and we returned to Esko excited about our good sales. We talked all the way back, planning for our next wagon on which we'd take even more. Abel told me my ideas had been wonderful, and he'd like me to accompany him each Saturday. I asked him about having Johann make some wooden boxes or dividers in which we could display our goods, and he liked that idea too.

That's exactly what Johann did, and he also painted a sign, "Heikkinen's Produce" to hang from the wagon. For the next trip Abel bought brown paper bags from the grocer in Esko. Our customers, who hadn't brought their own basket or box, seemed appreciative of that small bonus. Each Saturday after our sale, we'd count the dollars and coins we'd been paid. After the second Saturday Abel was easily able to pay for the wheels and axles for the wagon. He was relieved to be debt free again. Abel gave me the money my flowers and kitchen garden brought in, telling me to remember to shop for something I needed, and since we almost always stopped for supplies on Saturday, I enjoyed choosing thread or fabric, and sometimes something special to eat, such as an orange or two. Abel carefully recorded the money he was paid, as well as our expenses, in a ledger. He said he'd like to buy another cow or two but felt he should wait until after our second year of farming. All in all, he was delighted to be the owner of such a productive farm.

Our crops had been very prolific, due to good weather and rain, due to God, and good care due to all of us. Abel and Johann dug a fruit cellar, so we would be able to preserve our bounty over the winter. We often wondered what we would have done that first year without Johann. He felt like a talented young brother to both of us, and we wondered whether he would really leave after staying with us for a year.

Autumn was an especially beautiful time on our farm. We kept busy harvesting, preserving and selling. The men used scythes to cut hay and to cut down the rye, wheat, oats, and barley. We had stacks of drying hay in many spots. We all helped with the winnowing, separating the oats, wheat and barley from the chaff. Johann brought the wheat to the Palkie Grist Mill, returning with five 100 pound bags of flour. The charge for the grinding had been one bag of our flour. We suspected we had plenty of flour to supply bread for our family for the year.

Each time we brought our goods to market, we parked the wagon in the same place. Customers began looking for us and were waiting if we happened to be late. That made us feel good. Mikko got lots of attention, which he enjoyed. I would see some babies who were very shy, but Mikko seemed to love people. We marveled at his good health and steady growth.

Each day we kept noticing things we needed, mostly which we made, or did without. I suggested a cat to keep mice away, and that was easily remedied with our next trip to town. We found a beautiful calico kitten that we named "Kitty". Mikko loved the kitty but was too rough to be left alone with it.

We needed barrels, which Johann made and bought a few crocks, plus vinegar, for pickle making. Johann taught me how to make baskets from willow, an activity I learned to enjoy. My baskets were not as tight or well-shaped as Johann's, but were still serviceable. I began drying tomatoes and the herbs, as well as braiding onions together to hang them for drying. I had picked June berries, choke cherries, raspberries, blueberries, and strawberries earlier in the summer, and though we ate many fresh, I also had dozens of paraffin-covered jars of jam to brighten our winter diet and many other berries dried and stored in crocks in the root cellar. I brought in herb plants for the windowsills and looked forward to making curtains during the winter. Our little cottage looked homey, filled with our bounty and a healthy, happy family.

15

Joy Amongst Dreariness

"And the Word was made flesh and dwelt among us (and we beheld His glory, the glory as of the only begotten of the Father), full of glory and truth."

JOHN 1:14

Our first winter was hard, not because we didn't have food or shelter but because the days were so short and dreary, and our cottage seemed to grow smaller the longer we were confined inside. We knew the days had been even shorter in Finland, but none of us remembered winter seeming as long as it did in America. Abel said he needed more tools, especially for leather work, but he refused to spend any more of our savings. I missed a treadle sewing machine, feeling my hand sewing was simply not strong enough for making clothing. Johann, on the other hand, seemed able to do a great deal with his knife and plane. His hands were always busy.

I eagerly anticipated our first Christmas. Abel cut down a sweet little spruce tree which made our cottage smell wonderful even if it didn't have a decoration on it. I decorated our cottage with things from nature: pine cones, twig stars, bouquets of boughs and berries and lots of candles. I even used some of the apple slices I had dried as decorations, knowing the birds would enjoy them when we were done with them. Every other day in December I tried to make a Christmas treat and then put it in the fruit cellar so we wouldn't eat all of it. Packages wrapped in brown bags started appearing under the tree, and I learned I wasn't the only one anticipating Christmas.

We went to midnight Christmas Eve services. Even Johann came with us. The hymns, the candles, and the proclamation of Christ's birth ministered to all of us, except Mikko, who slept through the entire service. The bells rang at midnight as we tucked the blankets around us and happily made our way home in a sleigh Johann had built.

In the morning after a breakfast of cardamom bread and hot chocolate with whipped cream we exchanged gifts: I had knitted gray woolen socks for all three of "my men". Abel gave me a rabbit coin purse he had made for my gardening earnings and a hammer to Johann to start his carpentry tool set. He'd also made beautiful rabbit fur slippers for all of us. Johann had put his skills to good use, whittling a horse and wagon for Mikko, who immediately began chewing it, a set of covered wooden boxes for me to use in the kitchen, and nests in which the chickens could lay their eggs for Abel. He even remembered Kitty by attaching a whittled mouse to a deerskin cord. When he showed Mikko how to make it move for Kitty, Mikko laughed and laughed until we all did the same, with happy tears running down our cheeks.

We received a box from back home, packed with the bundle of clothing and linens I'd left behind, new pants and shirts for Mikko, which he badly needed, and a lovely embroidered tablecloth for our cottage.

With my family's gifts, Mumo had enclosed a letter, which I treasured:

More and more young folks are leaving Finland. They want land but also fear Russia will draft our young men again. We often say you made your big move at just the right time.

We are a year older but well. Your Ma and I have visited Silja a few times. She says she and Eero are overworked. The twins look mighty big and strong enough to take over lots of the farm work so I'm not sure what the problem is. She did say that Arvo and Margit have moved to Helsinki. Both are working and saving to buy fares to America. Rumor has it that Arvo is drinking. I hope he shapes up.

Your sisters and families are fine.

I've delivered five babies since you've been gone, but it doesn't look like your sisters will have any more. Instead it will have to be you.
I pray for the three of you daily.

Love,
Mumo

The gifts were wonderful, but the letter meant ever so much more. We really had been too busy to miss our family, but seeing Mumo's handwriting was a bittersweet reminder of her love.

Abel's father had not written but had send a box and Christmas card. The box contained a beautifully whittled horse for Mikko, a pocket watch for Abel, and a beautiful brooch, which we believed to be the last of Liisa's jewelry, for me. The gifts were symbolic of his love.

I had not planned well enough to send gifts, but I do remember clearly the short note I had sent home:

Dear Family:

We miss you folks but are doing well in America. The farm is prosper-
ing due to the blessings of God and our hard work. Mikko is a delightful
toddler, growing fast and learning lots. His enjoyment of the world makes
us laugh each day.

Our love,
Abel, Eva and Mikko

Johann had received a letter from his girlfriend and seemed to be walking on air. She was working as a maid in Helsinki and saving most of what she earned. It was obvious she was waiting to join him. Her letter must have motivated him to talk about leaving us. He said he hoped to send her money to help with her passage and wondered if Abel was able to give him any money to do so. My stomach churned to hear such a blunt question, but I should have known Abel had it figured out. Still, I was re-lieved when I heard Abel say he had put aside fifty dollars towards the fare, and Johann could have it whenever he wanted. Johann asked whether we thought he should send a money order or send the cash. To my relief, Abel suggested the money order and directions of how to purchase her ticket.

For the rest of the day, Johann sat at the table writing what must have been a most lengthy letter. The only time he stopped was to pay attention to Mikko, who had chosen the day to start walking around the table and chairs. He'd go all around the table until he got to Johann, who would scoop him up and tickle him, and then Mikko's journey would start all over again.

In honor of the day, Abel had butchered one of our chickens which I roasted with potatoes, carrots and onions. Along with fresh buns, butter, jam and my little selection of Finnish cookies and breads, we had a feast. At the end of the day Mikko's favorite word was cookie!

16

Endless Work

"Seek the LORD and His strength, seek His face continually."

1 CHRONICLES 16:11

The next day, after morning chores were done, Johann took his fifty dollars to the post office to send a money order to his sweetheart. When he returned he was excited and wanted to talk about the carpentry business he would start. We knew he was very skilled and worked hard so did not doubt that he'd be successful. He didn't know when Maija Liisa would arrive but would like to be prepared to move right after they were married. He didn't seem to have any idea of how to start his business.

Abel, wanting to show his faith in Johann, said he would like to invest five dollars in the business, with which he suggested Johann make samples of things he could take orders for. Johann was very appreciative and started dreaming of a small store, with an apartment above it. He talked excitedly about what he would build.

He asked what we needed made before he left, and I said a high chair for Mikko, and Abel said he'd like his help in building a sauna, close to the river. I said he should work on small items, like the beautiful boxes he made for me to have on display also. Johann had great energy and felt he could do all of that and more and also stay until the fields were planted. Abel had put down a cover crop of clover so felt planting would be much easier this year.

I will never say our first winter flew by, but we kept busy planning and working. Abel tended the livestock, happily announcing that both one of the sheep and one of the pigs was pregnant. The chickens continued to lay eggs, and Abel said he planned to buy chicks to enlarge his poultry flock. The cows contentedly yielded milk, which we drank and from which I made butter. Abel said he'd wait to see how next year's crops grew, and if he could afford to, wanted at least six more cows, knowing he could sell excess milk and cream to the Esko Creamery. How puzzling it was to me to realize no matter how much his farm yielded, Abel would want to produce more. Abel regularly hunted also, and venison and rabbits added variety to our meals, as well as providing deer hide and rabbit fur for many uses.

Mikko changed from a baby to a busy toddler during that first winter. He loved to run and had started to babble more and more. He could say Mama, Dada, Jo, and Kitty when we celebrated his first birthday in March, but his favorite words were cookie, again, more and no-no. He also loved to listen to the animal sounds and imitate them.

Spring came early with our last frost in early May. Johann heard from Maija-Liisa that she had bought her tickets and would arrive in July. Johann couldn't hide his disappointment that it would be so late, but finally got back to his cheerful self. Abel and I talked about letting them stay with us until they could find a place to rent, and we both felt it was not only the right thing to do, but would be good for all of us.

The 1918 planting began, and I knew I would only see the men for meals. I repeated the planting of my kitchen garden, increasing the amount of everything I'd planted the previous year, including the flowers. The days were warm and sunny, but there was little rain. Each morning Abel and Johann would fill all of our containers with river water and take them on the wagon to the fields. They'd use the water on the crops, sometimes repeating the hauling process up to 20 times in a day. I took care of my watering by using the pump. By July the water from the pump lessened to a trickle, and we knew we couldn't use it any more, so water for my garden and for the household also needed to be hauled. The hauling of water was back breaking work, but it was necessary for the crops to survive. We watered steadily every day but Sunday, and the plants grew surprisingly strong and healthy. Along with milking, meals, laundry, and caring for Mikko, I began picking strawberries, which I mostly made into jams, and just about when I was caught up with them, raspberries, blueberries, peas and beans were ripe. I suppose it was the warm days that made everything ready so much earlier.

The first day we'd packed the wagon with vegetables, fruit and flowers was the day Mr. Wirtanen brought Maija-Liisa to the farm. She had arrived by train the night before and walked to the General Store just as Johann had instructed her to do. When Johann came to the wagon with his last load of vegetables and saw Maija-Liisa, he put the box down, picked up his girl, and swung her in his arms. I don't remember ever seeing anyone look so happy. They whooped and hollered, and we decided to make our trip to West Duluth and leave them alone.

Our sales went better than ever since most farmers were having their crops dry up, and even with a short stop at the store for ice we were home before noon eager to tell Johann how well our morning had gone. Things had gone even better for Johann who had walked with Maija-Lisa to the Justice of the Peace and had been married. My plans for their wedding and reception evaporated, but recognizing their happiness, I couldn't be disappointed for long.

After much discussion between the four of us adults, it was decided that Johann and Maija-Liisa would stay with us at least through August, giving them time to find a place to rent and begin their carpentry business as well as giving us help with watering. We were not worried about an end date, but Johann insisted that they would be gone by fall.

Many times at night, Abel and I would agree that it was a blessing the young couple was staying with us. They were easy to be around, more than willing to help, which was important during our dry summer when watering was the only way to keep the crops alive. Also, as Mikko's need to be supervised increased, I was at a low in energy due to being pregnant once again (for which we were very happy) and having severe morning sickness (for which no one was happy). Nevertheless, the summer flew with all of us working from sun up to sun down. Maija (Johann had shortened her name, and we all followed suit) had never worked on a farm or taken care of children, but she was eager to learn and tried ever so hard. She was fascinated to see how vegetables grew, and how milk and eggs were gathered, but she was absolutely mesmerized by little Mikko, who was in a whirlwind stage. As we worked together, she endlessly asked questions about being a wife and mother. She was so sincere and complimentary that it was a joy to be with her.

Wagon load after wagon load went to West Duluth and some was even purchased by the local grocer. At the end of August, we had earned three times as much as the previous summer and had at least a month left of sales. Johann was sending some of his wooden projects with us, and we took orders for them. He was selling rockers, boxes, toys, and many implements, especially wooden spoons. In early September Johann and Maija found a small storefront with an apartment above to rent in East Duluth. We took the wagon into Duluth, stopped at a lumber yard, where he had arranged to buy lumber and a few tools in exchange for building furniture for the owner, and sadly delivered them to their new home. After hugs, tears, and promises of seeing them each of the next several Saturdays when he'd deliver his projects and collect his new orders and payments, we were off to save the remaining crops.

I had never seen so many tomatoes ripening at one time, and I began sun drying them along with beans. Onions were braided and hanging everywhere and potatoes were drying off in the sun. We thought about going into West Duluth twice a week, but we were afraid we couldn't keep up with the need for moisture if we gave up two mornings, the best time of the day to water, so instead filled our wagon higher than ever and also sold more produce to the Esko Grocery Store. We found if we put our produce in gunny sacks we could stack them very high and quickly put them in display boxes when we arrived in Duluth.

And so it went all through the month of September, working extremely hard but realizing profit from it. We had one marvelous day of rain, and we put all of our containers on the ground to be filled by the miraculous moisture. Much to our disappointment, there were only puddles in the bottom of the pails, BUT for a few hours we had FELT relieved.

Abel hauled the water, and I distributed it on the plants, prioritizing with the most vulnerable, the tomatoes, peppers, and cucumbers, and then going on to the rest. The oats, rye, and barley had full heads a month earlier than the previous year, and we were delighted to cut them down, knowing we wouldn't have to water them again. Row by row we harvested, filling gunny sacks with produce, which Abel brought to the fruit cellar. One day he told me I should move our valuables down there also, as he'd heard that many farms had been robbed. Times were hard for the town families who didn't have the room or knowledge to grow their own food and had to spend more than usual to buy it.   Consequently, I did take our clothes and linens from Finland, my notebooks, our family Bible, and a few of the beautiful pieces Johann had made into the fruit cellar, and Abel, after carefully counting it, hid our income in a hole he had dug there also.

Our one relief from our hard work was found in the sauna that Johann had built just as he had promised he would do. It was a small building with a dressing room attached. Abel had bought a small stove to heat the sauna, and then in a creative way to use the rock from the fields, Johann had cemented them to both the inside and outside of the wooden frame. Our little rock sauna was beautiful and heated up quickly. Nothing felt better after a long day's work than sitting on the sauna benches, throwing water on the rock-covered stove and sweating away our aches—and cares. We would use scrub brushes to clean our bodies and wash each other's backs. Sometimes we would use cedar or birch switches, which gave off a wonderful fragrance and stimulated our skin. The whole process was followed by a dip into the river, where the cold water rinsed us off and refreshed us.

We continued our gathering and preserving as well as selling throughout September and into October. We even had a beautiful pumpkin and squash crop that had had plenty of time to ripen and was quickly purchased. We kept planning to buy a braided rug for our cottage, but never seemed to be able to take the time to go to Cloquet to do so.

Fall, usually my favorite time of the year, seemed dangerously dry. Whatever was not watered shriveled up and died. Even small trees were dying while the roots of larger ones could find water in the earth. We heard rumors of fire, and in October there was frequently the smell of smoke in the air.

When we woke up on October 10, the smell of smoke was even stronger than usual. The sky was totally gray, but not with the promise of rain. We went about our day-- for some reason working in silence. After lunch, Abel said he would ride into town to learn what was going on. Feeling very tired, I told him I was going to take a nap with Mikko. I remember clearly Abel kissing us both good-bye and saying his usual "sweet dreams."

17

Fire!

"Thou art my hiding place; thou shalt preserve me from trouble...."

Psalm 32:7

I woke up to the sound of Mikko talking to himself. "Did you wake up before me, my little man?" He just smiled as he played with his blocks. He was wearing the overalls that Mumo had made for him and often pointed to himself and said "Mikko man".

I quickly realized that it was very dark, which confused me because I didn't believe I could have slept all day. Besides, Abel was not inside. Just as I was trying to figure out what time it was, I heard Abel's horse galloping up to the house.

"Eva! Eva! You must leave. There's a fire heading our way." With the smoke in the air we had talked about what we would do in case of fire, so I wasn't surprised to see Abel hitching the wagon to his horse and bringing it down to a wide part of the river. He returned to the house and together we pulled furniture and rugs out to the nearest empty field. He told me to pen up the chickens and bring them to the wagon and then go to the river with Mikko.

The chickens were uncooperative but I got four of them in the crate. As I was concentrating on them, Mikko stood in our cottage doorway, saying "Mikko help?" and then, "Look, Mama. Look at the light." I turned to where he was pointing and was shocked to see our stand of pines going up in flames.

Abel came back on his horse. "Forget the chickens! Get Mikko and yourself to the river!"

I scooped up my little boy and started running to the river. The ground felt strangely hot to my bare feet. I should have taken the time to put on my shoes, but it was too late.

"Mama, Mama, where's Kitty?"

"She'll be okay, Mikko. She's probably hiding."

"Kitty okay," he solemnly announced.

As I came to the path to the river, I considered stopping at the sauna. Surely the rock walls would protect us. A terrible roar changed my mind.

My hair had come unbraided while I napped and it kept catching on the brush close to the path. There was another roar, and I pulled away from the brush and kept running. It was too smoky to see what was ahead of us, but I knew my way well enough. I reached the water, knowing the wagon would be downstream. The water must have been cold, but I didn't even feel it. Instead I thrashed through the water, losing my balance a few times and finally falling face first. I desperately reached for my precious little boy who was sputtering, but still said, "No Mama. Too cold to swim."

Much to my relief Abel's strong hands reached out for Mikko. I don't know where he had come from but was ever so thankful. I knew he was saying something, but I couldn't hear his words above the roar, so simply followed him, holding on to his overalls. Without Mikko in my arms I was able to walk faster and within minutes we were at the wagon, which held 3 sheep and a bawling cow, and much to my surprise, Kitty. Abel lifted up Mikko and then boosted me as I clambered onto the wagon. He said close to my ear, "I'll go see if I can save any more of our animals."

"God keep you safe," I said, wondering if I would even see him again.

The fire snapped and roared on all sides of us. Trees were crashing into the river and sizzling as they reached the water. Mikko was coughing terribly as the smoke thickened. I sat shivering on the wagon with Mikko on my lap. He was so concerned for the animals and the panicky noises they made. "We're all right. Jesus will take care of us," he kept saying in an attempt to comfort all of us.

It was like a nightmare, but I knew we would not wake up from it. I wondered how long the fire would last and was glad I couldn't see the damage being done. I mourned for our little farm, knowing that our cottage, which was close to the stand of pines, would no doubt be lost. With good fortune, the barns and sauna would stand. I grieved over my husband's hard work and the great loss he would feel. We were fortunate to have sold so much of our crops and to have put much in the root cellar. Would that be spared? As the fire raged on, I doubted anything would be left standing.

And then I began to pray like I had never prayed before. I begged God to spare our little farm. We'd come to America with faith that God would protect us. Sometime during my pleading I realized how blessed we'd been. We had made it to America safely and had been blessed with assistance from Johann. We had food and money in our root cellar and could rebuild again. At least some of our livestock was safe as evidenced by the bawling sheep and cow right beside me. I thanked God for protecting Abel, Mikko and me. The more I prayed, the calmer I became. The fire had traveled to both sides of the river, and the smoke became blacker and thicker as even green brush and plants on shore went up in flames. Little Mikko coughed and coughed, and I was thankful he'd forget this horrid experience. I lay down on the wagon and had Mikko lie beside me, showing him how to breathe at the small gaps between the boards, where the air was not smoky. I don't know whether it helped or not since he still coughed, but I did not know what else to do. I held on to him, patting him and saying comforting words he couldn't possibly hear. We were safe and simply had to wait till the fire passed and Abel came to get us. I wondered whether he'd been able to save any of the animals or had borne the cruelty of seeing them burn to death.

I don't know how much time passed. Ridiculous as it seems, I dozed off. I woke with a start and then relaxed as soon as I saw my sleeping son. I could see small fires in many places but none of the wild inferno of earlier. I leaned against the cow that had finally calmed enough to lie down. The animals seemed to have survived. Even Kitty was curled up by Mikko. I dipped into the river and drank deeply from the muddy water. I thanked the Lord for sparing us. Where was Abel? Why hadn't he returned? The thought of losing the man I loved was impossible to comprehend, and yet the thought kept entering my head. I used my skirt dipped into water to wipe off my face, but instead of bringing cooling, it stung terribly. It must have burned at some time. I selfishly picked up Mikko and held him close to me, knowing he was sleeping soundly but that I needed him. The deafening noise had stopped. In fact it was eerily quiet until I heard splashing of water. And then, to my relief, I saw Abel and two other men on horses, appearing like ghosts from the thick smoke. It seemed so strange to me that they were riding in the river, and then it dawned on me that the ground was probably too hot for the horses to bear.

"We've been rescued, Mikko! We're safe. Thank the Lord." The men looked worn out as they checked the wagon to see if they could move it. One of our neighbors said, "It sure is good to find survivors," and then tears flowed down his cheeks, leaving trails on his sooty face. Did that mean he'd lost someone?

Abel told me there was a wagon on the road that would take us to the armory in Duluth. "We're okay," I said as I realized how badly my throat and the rest of my body ached. Someone took Mikko from my hands, and Abel pulled me up in front of him on his horse. We rode a short distance to the bridge, where there was a covered wagon with a red cross on it being pulled by two horses.

Men lifted me gently into the wagon which held six cots, each holding a fire victim. I sat on the floor with Mikko on my lap. A young women also was in the wagon, helping the patients. She offered me a cup of water which I accepted gratefully. "I'll see you soon," Abel promised. I could only nod to him.

18

Beyond Belief

"Eva, he's gone."

We were brought to the armory, a large building in the East end of Superior Street. Military cots had been put up. Once I answered as many questions as I could, I was led to a cot I'd share with Mikko. Nurses, doctors, and soldiers milled around. Before long, a gentle young woman removed my burnt clothing and washed me. Even her gentle touch was almost unbearable. Mikko did not appear to be burned, but he continued to cough. The nurse pointed to his chest and to a nearby doctor. Though I didn't want to be separated from him, I did not have the strength to follow and was surprised that Mikko did not fuss. What seemed like a long time later, he was returned to me. Somehow food was distributed, but neither Mikko nor I was hungry. We did accept water, and Mikko, who had been weaned for months, asked to nurse. I knew my breasts wouldn't have any milk, but he seemed soothed all the same.

I awoke hours later, and Mikko was gone. When a nurse passed by, I tried to ask her where he was, but she didn't understand. Finally, I spotted the nurse who had been extremely gentle with Mikko and me. I stood by my cot, but when I tried to walk to her, my legs would not hold me. The crash of my falling alerted the nurse, and she came to me. I knew she understood my questions, but she seemed to ignore them. Finally when she had me back in bed I said as loudly as I could "Mikko!"

"Eva, he's gone. His lungs had been destroyed by the fire. We couldn't save him."

My little boy couldn't be dead. I heard someone screaming and finally realized the screams were coming from me. The nurse gave me a shot, and I fell asleep, comprehending nothing.

19

Emptiness

Just let me die.

When I awoke I was tied to a bed in a large room that smelled of burnt flesh and urine. A nurse came to me and started asking questions in English, but her language was no more foreign than the room I was in or my state of mind. I had no desire to live. I was relieved I was bound because it eliminated the need for me to try to do anything.

My days were a series of black and white: black when I closed my eyes and white when I opened them to see white walls, white blankets and people dressed in white. I remember being given water and someone feeding me broth. Other beds must have held patients, but I had no interest in them.

Abel came to see me. He held my hand, and we sobbed.

Our pastor came and prayed at my bedside, I had no understanding of a God who would allow my little boy to die, so the pastor's words meant nothing.

There was both a Finnish doctor, who came weekly, and a Finnish nurse who stopped often. They asked questions which made no more sense than the English ones did. They always asked how I felt. I said nothing rather than telling the truth: *I felt nothing. I didn't want to feel anything. Just let me die.*

I could feel the baby moving inside me. I was sorry it was still alive. Why should it struggle so hard to be born when it would only die?

One day I heard the doctor talking to Abel. I heard him say "nervous breakdown" and "prevent her from hurting the baby."

One day I heard the pastor talking to Abel. He mentioned "time to heal" and "prayers". What foolishness!

One day I heard the nurse talking to Abel. She said I'd get better but would never get over my great loss. For the first time in days I felt something—maybe not quite fondness—but I appreciated that she understood.

Days passed by in a blur, but the darkness did not lift. I swallowed when I was fed, stood when I was helped up, sat when I was put in a chair, but nothing more. I was alive but not living. I saw nothing and everything through a dark cloud as thick and oppressive as the smoke I'd somehow lived through. There was no purpose, no hope. As far as I was concerned, my life was over.

And then one day when Abel came, I was sitting in a chair. He said nothing, just held my hand while he knelt by the chair. When I looked at him, tears were running down his cheeks, and I knew I had to help this man I loved. It became crystal clear to me that he had lost even more than me: his son, his farm, and his wife. I kissed his filthy hair and whispered in my raspy voice, "Take me home."

He looked at me with surprised blue eyes. "I can't, Eva, but I want to, and I will as soon as I can."

It was not the answer I expected or wanted, but it was enough. It was as if a small flame had been lit inside me, and I knew I could and would get better. Never well, but better. My motivation was Abel. He needed me, and I had to get home.

As I started on my journey of healing, I noticed and responded to things around me. When a spoon of food was brought to my mouth, I took it with my hand and fed myself. I said thank you to anyone who did anything for me. I looked at each person I saw and often managed to say hello. My doctor told me my vocal chords had been damaged by inhaling smoke, but that eventually my voice should return.

When our pastor came on his regular visit, I listened politely and even thanked him though I knew what he said made no sense.

When the doctor came, I answered his questions, trying hard to say what he wanted to hear. When he asked me if there was anything I needed, I asked if I could wash my hair, if I could have a notebook and pencil, and if I could take a walk.

"You're making progress, Eva. I'll see what I can do."

The next day I was allowed to bathe and wash my hair. Though there was a nurse standing by me the whole time, the warm water and soap felt wonderful. I was given clothes to wear, and I wondered whose they were. The nurse told me they were now mine, and it felt good not to be in a gown. When I looked in the mirror to brush my hair, I was shocked. My long hair was now just stubble and a grayish color. My eyebrows and eyelashes were starting to grow back, and I could see that most of my skin had peeled away, and the new skin was bright red. My face, especially my eyes did not look like mine. They looked like they belonged to someone very old or very ill. I had never been so thin and the healthy bulge of our unborn baby didn't seem to fit at all.

When I asked for shoes, I was given slippers instead, but that would be all right for now while my feet continued to heal. My progress was slow, painful, and often seemed to be going backwards. I experienced a bone-deep weariness, but I felt the hope of returning to Abel and our home.

He came every Sunday and mostly just sat beside me. There simply was nothing to say. He did tell me I was looking much better. When I looked at him, I could tell he had lost weight. His face was drawn, and there were wrinkles I hadn't noticed before, but I didn't tell him what I saw. I asked him to bring one of the notebooks Mumo had given me, and he brought it the next week. In the meantime I walked as much as I could, becoming familiar with every corner of the hospital. My favorite room, the craft room, had tables and chairs and shelves full of crafts, puzzles, games, and books. It was there I found the pencil I needed to write in my notebook, and I hid it in my pocket—with no guilt. I also knitted socks for Abel and myself.

The next time the doctor came he found me in the craft room knitting booties. He must have thought that was a very good sign because he smiled broadly as he asked me about my pregnancy. He said he wanted me to deliver the baby at the hospital. I hid my disappointment at those words, knowing that much could happen before January when the baby was due.

I knew I was still very weak, and I forced myself to eat the meals and snacks that were offered though I didn't even taste them. I drank my milk and asked for cream in my coffee. I asked my favorite nurse, Hanna, if there was anything I could do to help at the hospital. She put me in charge of keeping the craft room orderly and introduced me to another Finn who didn't seem to have any visitors. I found out from her that she had lost her husband and two daughters in the fire. She lived in Kettle River about 30 miles from Cloquet, and that's why none of her neighbors or pastor came to see her. She told me she was going to return to Finland as soon as she had the money and was well enough to travel. She had such a sad story to tell that I was embarrassed that I felt so sorry for myself.

Nights were still the worst for me. I continued to wake from nightmares about the fire. I was always running with Mikko but never ran fast enough. In one horrible dream my long hair was caught in tree branches, and Mikko would not leave me. I'd lie awake wondering what I could have done differently, how I could have saved my little boy. I didn't even know when he had died. I relived that afternoon over and over again, always wondering why he had died and not me.

In the daylight I usually became a little hopeful. I remembered all the trips Abel, Mikko and I had made to West Duluth with our wagon loads of produce. It had seemed a short trip, and I knew I could walk it. I needed winter wear and good boots and began to plan how I would get them. I asked Hanna if she thought I could walk outside to get some fresh air. She said she would ask my doctor, and he approved it as long as I dressed warmly and limited my walks to an hour. I was thrilled, and before I could even ask her, Hanna said she would go to the Salvation Army Store to find clothing for me. The next day she came with a wool hat, scarf and mittens. They didn't match but looked warm. The next week she found socks and shoes, but the shoes hurt my feet. She said she couldn't find a woman's coat or boots. I told her I wouldn't mind if the coat and boots were for a man, thinking to myself they might disguise me as a small man. The next day she had with her sturdy boots and a long man's woolen coat. I was thrilled and went on my first walk that afternoon. It was windy, and I found out I couldn't walk more than a few blocks, but it felt good, and I knew I would get stronger.

On Sunday when Abel returned I told him I was walking, and he and I went outside together. I innocently asked him how far it was from the hospital to our home, and he told me about 12 miles. "Do you still go the way we did when we brought the vegetables to market?" I asked.

"Ya, that's what I do," he replied.

"Well, thank you for coming," I said, not wanting him to become suspicious of my plans.

The next three weeks I walked every day except one when we had near blizzard conditions. The combination of eating more, exercising, and having a plan was making me stronger each day. The doctor was very pleased with my progress, and told me to keep doing whatever I was doing. I wondered what he would think if I told him I was hiding food from my dinner tray and then asking for more. No one had refused me a second serving of bread or cheese or fruit. Milk came in little glass bottles. I wanted to have two of them with me when I left but would have to wait until that day to take them.

Thanksgiving came, and the hospital had a turkey dinner. The weather was fairly mild for the end of November, and I decided I would leave the next day. At breakfast I stuffed my pockets with food, including two milks I boldly took from the milk cart. I told Hanna I would like to walk a little longer since I'd eaten so much on Thanksgiving. She handed me an apple, a doughnut, and a milk to take with. I smiled to myself as I bundled up, realizing I hadn't needed to be a thief. I left the front door, as usual, feeling as if I was escaping from prison, but this time I had no plans of returning.

20

The Endless Walk

I had been raised to have Sisu. I could not give up.

The day was crisp and beautiful. The sun was shining in a brilliant blue sky. I started west on Grand Avenue and then North on Cody Avenue, walking up the hill with little problem. The higher I walked, the better my view of Lake Superior was. Its beautiful blue somehow encouraged me. I easily made it to the village of Proctor, a bustling railroad town. I turned off before I came to the main street, wanting to avoid anyone's curiosity. I doubted the hospital staff would look for me in this direction, if they even looked, but would avoid a return to the hospital at all cost.

When the sun was overhead, I took a break, eating my doughnut and drinking two of my bottles of milk. Occasionally, someone would walk by as I sat on a bench, but no one as much as nodded to me. I heard the noon whistle blow, and many workers poured out of the railroad roundhouse. As some were walking towards the benches, no doubt to eat their lunch, I began on my way. The walking was easier now that I had food in my stomach and was not walking uphill.

I turned on the Stark Road, actually enjoying my exercise, and rejoicing that in a few hours I would be with Abel. I knew he would be surprised, but I was also sure he would be pleased. He couldn't deny that I was physically well if I could walk these twelve miles, and he had begun to believe I was mentally well a few weeks ago. I would have a month to help him fix up whatever ruins the fire had left, and then I'd prepare for our baby. I made a mental list of the things I would need for the first time realizing that the nappies, gowns, and blankets I'd used for Mikko were probably reduced to ashes. Abel had told me that the Red Cross had delivered lumber to farms that had been burned, so I expected he'd repaired our cottage enough to make it habitable. And we did have a root cellar filled with food as well as our income from the fall market. I marveled at Abel's foresight in burying his income. I reminisced about our life before the fire and realized how wonderful it had been.

And then I began thinking about Mikko and how precious he had been. It was still too painful to think of him, so instead I practiced the English words I'd learned in the hospital: please, thank you, hello, good-bye, my name is Eva Heikkinen, yes, no, water, coffee, fire, and boy. What a sad handful of words!

I felt as if I were slowing down and made an attempt to speed up. I looked carefully at the land I passed, imagining who lived in the houses. There was no sign of fire here. As I continued on the Stark Road, crossing the Midway Road I knew I was well over halfway home. The sky was clouding up, but at the rate I was walking, I would beat any snow.

I took an apple from my pocket and also felt the notebook Mumo had given me. I had written a great deal while I was in the hospital and didn't want to leave my words behind. Maybe when I became even stronger, I would read what I had written, and maybe I'd begin to understand. At the moment, I knew it would be too painful. Once again I realized there would always be an ache in my heart, an incomplete part of me, after losing our little boy.

It began to snow lightly. Large snowflakes floated down, and I caught many on my tongue, enjoying the cool moisture. That gave me the idea of filling my empty milk bottle with snow. If I put it in my skirt pocket, my body heat would melt it, and I'd have water. Somehow I think I'd been taught that eating snow made you thirstier.

On I went, step after step. I was tired and thirsty, but remembered I had been raised to have Sisu. I could not give up. Occasionally, a horse-drawn wagon would pass or meet me, and once even one of the new-fangled Model T's met me. If there were trees close by, I'd duck behind them, not wanting anyone to notice me.

I crossed a railroad track and thought of following it rather than the road, but I could not be sure it was the same track going through our stand of pines, so I kept walking on the road.

I saw more farms, a few crows, lots of trees, and some cattle in the fields. I knew I could do this, but I did need to rest—just for a few minutes. I noticed a stump and sat upon it after taking my snow water out of my skirt pocket. I was surprised by what a small amount of water it had become but drank it greedily. Next I drank the rest of my milk, leaving only my last apple left.

It felt so good to be sitting. I slipped down from the stump and leaned against it. That took away all the pressure I'd felt on my back, and I felt my body relax. I'd close my eyes for a few moments and then start the last stretch of my walk......

21

Going Home

"Yea, though I walk through the valley of the shadow of death, I will fear no evil; for thou art with me; thy rod and thy staff they comfort me."

PSALMS 23:4

I woke with a start, feeling stiff and cold. The bright morning in which I'd started my walk was long gone, replaced by blowing snow and near darkness. I had made a disastrous mistake. I got to my feet and reached the road, feeling the task ahead was impossible. The short rest that was supposed to have refreshed me had turned into a deep sleep that left me groggy and listless.

My feet were numb, and it took all of my will to force them to move. One step at a time. I couldn't give up now. I was only a mile or two from my goal. I was terribly angry with God. Why would he do this to me? Wasn't taking Mikko enough retribution for Him? Apparently not. Now He would let me freeze in a ditch, a short walk from Abel.

What would Hanna think? Would she forever blame herself for equipping me with winter clothes and letting me leave. Would the doctor think of my actions as irrational ones of the insane? And then I thought of Abel. Would he remember me asking him to take me home? Would he blame himself for one more death?

With those thoughts, I shook off my lethargy. I had to make it. I had to. One foot in front of the other. Again and again and again. I knew I was walking in the right direction though I could see nothing I recognized.

I shook my fist at God in anger and blame. Why, God, why? You brought us over the ocean and let us settle in a beautiful place. You brought other people into our life, who we helped and who helped us. You gave us a son, who was beautiful and innocent. He trusted you. He could have done so much with his good mind and body. Do you enjoy teasing us with such blessings and then ripping them away? Is it a game to you when you're bored? I put into words thoughts that must have been boiling deep inside me.

I will not let you end me this way. I will not let you hurt Abel again. Almost immediately I tripped, falling onto my face, which was scraped and cut by ice and gravel. Blood ran down my face, running into my eyes, and all my arguments came to an end. All right, Lord, I have no power. You've shown me again. It was pride that made me think I could do this. It was pride that had me question your goodness. I am sorry my God. All my life I've believed in Jesus, your son, who died for me and my sins. Dear God, forgive my bullheadedness. Forgive me for deceiving the people at the hospital and Abel. Forgive me for stealing the food and the pencil. Forgive me for hating Silja and resenting her sons.

I know I am going to die. I can't even see where I'm walking. There's no light. I can't find my way. I'll keep walking, but I don't even know if I'm going the right direction. Forgive me, dear Lord, and take me to heaven to be with my little boy.

— ~

I was still lost, still tired, but I felt a peace I hadn't felt since before the fire, maybe not even since we had decided to go to America. I had ignored God. I had prayed, but I hadn't studied His Word, and sometimes on Sundays I'd felt too busy and not gone to church. And think how rude I'd been to our pastor when he visited me. I didn't listen to him. I didn't pray with him. But it was all right now. Suddenly a warmth came over me as I realized I wasn't the only one who had lost my only son. God knew what loss was. He had voluntarily given up His only son to suffer and die. Thank you, my Heavenly Father. He was Mikko's Heavenly Father also. He who knows when a sparrow falls must have also cried when His beautiful little Mikko, created by Him, suffered and died. What had Mikko said on the wagon during the fire? "Jesus will take care of us." Maybe he had been talking to me and not the animals.

Everything was all right. I was born into a culture of Sisu. I had used it all my life, but now I was helpless. If God let me die, it was all right. My struggling would end, and I would be with Mikko. If by some miracle He brought me to Abel, it would be His miracle, and I would live the rest of my life recognizing His great love. It was as if a great weight had left my heart. If I died, it was all right. And if by some miracle, I survived, that was all right too.

I kept walking, accepting I could not go much further. Without any visual guides, I occasionally fell into the ditch. Blood continued to run down my face. Then it was if someone said to me to walk in the middle of the road, as far from the ditch as possible. It would be much easier for my body to be found. Abel wouldn't have to wonder what had happened to me. So I slowly walked down the middle of the road, knowing I would not live through the night.

And then the most wonderful thing happened. I saw a light, a moving light ahead of me, and I walked toward it. I could not figure out what I was seeing. It was too dark and snowy for anyone to be out on a horse, but I continued to walk until I reached just that: a man on a horse. I don't know what he had done with the lantern I had seen, but he got down from his horse and asked me if I was Eva Heikkinen. When I nodded, he said, "Let's get you home. He helped me on the horse, and he mounted the saddle behind me. The horse was very large, but ever so gentle. The man continued on in the direction I'd been coming from and almost immediately turned onto the road on which I'd lived, which meant I had completely missed our turn-off.

He turned onto our driveway. I saw no light where our cottage had been but thought I saw one in our sauna. The man didn't hesitate. He rode right up to the sauna door and helped me down. I tried to open the door, but couldn't. It felt as if it were locked, but our sauna had never had a lock. Nevertheless, I knocked on the door, and after a bit, I heard Abel ask, "Who's there?" When I answered with my name, he opened the door, and I fell into his arms.

22

Home

"The angel of the LORD encampeth round about them that fear Him, and delivereth them."

PSALM 34:7

"How did you get here?" he asked.

"I walked but missed our turn off. Oh wait," I said, remembering my manners, and opened the door to thank my Good Samaritan. He was gone, but there was a crate at the door with some writing on it.

I couldn't make sense of anything but soon realized that there were animals in the sauna and a crudely made wooden attachment. The stove was lit, and it felt wonderfully warm. Even the sounds and smells of the animals were comforting.

"I'm so tired, Abel. Let's go to our cottage."

Abel looked so sad as he said, "It's gone. Everything's gone but this building. I told you, Eva, you couldn't come home."

"But Abel, I'm here, and I'm here to stay."

I don't know what he was thinking, but at that moment, I could only feel the relief of not perishing on the road and of being with him. "I can answer all of your questions tomorrow, but for now I need water and sleep." He held me for the longest time before giving me water and then helping me take off my coat and boots. My feet, cheeks, and fingertips were frost bitten, but only mildly. They would be all right. He cleaned my face of blood and rubble and led me to a makeshift cot, tucking blankets around me. I was shivering violently and when Abel saw it, he told me it would be crowded but he would join me. The warmth from his body was one of the best things I'd ever felt. I could only tell Abel I loved him before my heavy eyelids closed, and I slept.

Morning came with the sounds of the cows and the horse in the attached lean-to and pigs, lambs and chickens close to me. Abel told me to stay in bed, but my bladder disagreed, so I went outside to relieve myself, only to remember there was no outhouse. What I saw shocked me. Our trees and our buildings were all gone. I was thankful for the snow still coming down and covering the scarred land. I had to squat in the snow to release my waters. When I returned inside, Abel tucked me back in bed, and I did not resist. I watched him feed and water the animals. He disappeared for a while and returned with a bucket of steaming milk, which he poured in jars and put outside. Then he made oatmeal and coffee. We sat side by side on the cot, eating our food. The coffee was hot and strong, just like I liked it. As we sat there, I looked around at the building in which Abel had spent the last seven weeks. The animals looked well cared for, but Abel's little corner was so messy, I didn't know how he could find anything.

We sat quietly in no hurry since there was little we could do. Finally Abel said, "It's good to have you with me."

"So you're not mad at me?"

"No, not at all. I don't understand what made you leave a safe, clean place to come here though."

"I already told you, Abel, I need to be with you."

There was a long pause until he finally said, "I believe I need you more."

Again, we sat quietly. It seemed we'd said all that was necessary. Many minutes later, Abel said, "I see you looking around. What are you thinking?"

"I'm trying to figure out how to make the sauna more livable."

"And what have you thought of?"

"Not much. But maybe a shelf above the stove and hooks for our things."

"I learned enough from Johann to manage that," he smiled. Next week I'll need to buy supplies, and I can get a hammer and nails. Can you wait that long?"

I smiled shyly, knowing I could wait.

The next few days passed slowly but pleasantly. One day when Abel returned from the cows, carrying milk, he went right back outside and returned carrying a hefty crate with my name on it. I looked at the handwriting: Eva Heikkinen, Esko, but didn't recognize it. When I asked Abel where it came from, he only shrugged, "I don't know. I saw it today, but it could have been there yesterday already."

When we opened it, I found another miracle. In the wooden crate were two heavy quilts, bed sheets, a beautiful blue nightgown, and ladies' underwear. Below that was a man's shirt and pants, socks and underwear. And in the very bottom of the box were nappies, two flannel baby saques, and three blankets for our baby. There was a note at the very bottom:

> Eva,
>   We know the fire destroyed everything you had. We thought you could use these things. We're glad you made it home.
>
> Your sister in Christ,
> Hanna

I was so touched by Hanna's generosity I didn't even try to figure out how she had learned I had made it home. The items were nicer than anything we had and would be put to good use.

Abel went to town a few days later, returning with rye krisp, coffee, sugar, oatmeal, yeast, smoked pork hocks, dry peas, baking soda, the needed hammer and nails, and a silly, but lovely surprise, a black puppy, which he'd held in his coat all the way home. My immediate reaction was how difficult it would be to feed another mouth, but because of Abel's happiness, I held the thought in. He had another reason to be happy. He had stopped at the Red Cross to tell them I was home and was given more clothing for me, bars of soap, towels and sewing supplies. Best of all, he was given a new rifle and ammunition, which should mean our food supply would increase.

━ ～

With clothes we could wear (and clothes I could wash), we went to church learning that though the church building had been spared from the fire, the congregation by no means was untouched. We were welcomed, Mikko's death was mourned, and our survival was celebrated. We were even asked our needs, especially with a baby coming soon. Before we left that day the pastor's wife gave us a bundle of clothing. We were touched by the kindness and caring of our Christian brothers and sisters. We learned of other casualties—16 adults and 3 children in the area of Esko had been killed and injuries were many. I learned that Cloquet and Kettle River had been destroyed. I heard many horror stories until I couldn't listen any more. Rather I focused on conversations about the congregation planning to help rebuild homes and barns that had been burned. Several men talked to Abel, offering to lend to him their plows and wagons or whatever else was needed now or in the spring.

We were not alone—not that we ever had been, but it was ever so good to be reminded of it. The next two weeks were joyful. Here we were mourning our son and living with livestock, but we were at peace, thankful to be alive and once again hopeful.

— —

Abel was making plans. He had not heard from Johann since the fire but would try to hire him to rebuild the cottage and barns in the spring. This time we could pay him right away, so it possibly could help all of us. He thought we would be able to get more clothing and supplies from the Salvation Army or Red Cross. The wooden handles for his plow would have to be replaced, and we would have to buy a wagon. He asked if I still had my notebooks, and when I told him I had one with me, he asked to use a page on which to write things down.

Watching him write down his plans filled me with even more hope. We were once again looking towards the future.

Very quickly, we developed a comfortable routine of caring for the few animals, cooking and eating our simple meals, and firing the stove. Abel hauled water from the river for the animals and our household needs and hunted almost every day while I prepared meals and did the little cleaning that was necessary. Once he had shot a deer and a few rabbits he had butchering and tanning to do also,

Each day we walked the perimeter of our land. Moosti (Blackie) would start out scampering beside us, but soon his short, puppy legs would wear out, and he would whimper until one of us picked him up.

Every time I saw the remains of our forest I was reminded of the huge flames that had engulfed it. There was not a remnant left of anything but the sauna. We began to plan where we would rebuild the cottage, the outhouse, and the barns. The land, which had been sheltered by beautiful trees, was now very open and barren. Instead of seeing it as a disadvantage, Abel pointed out we could choose a variety of trees, the open fields would be easy to plow, and the ash had probably enriched the soil.

I couldn't make myself look at the river yet, so we kept away from it on our walks. We did walk along the road, and I started bringing a knife with to cut willow, so I could start replacing our baskets.

Our life was temporarily filled with leisure. We had time to rest and enjoy a comfortable companionship. We had only one lantern, so during the long evenings, we sat close together while I wove or wrote, and Abel started to make slippers from the rabbit fur.

23

A Christmas Surprise

"His mercy is on those who fear Him from generation to generation."

LUKE 1:50

Sooner than seemed possible, Abel reminded me he would need to go for supplies again. Without a wagon he could haul only a small amount of feed needed by the livestock. He said he would have to figure out a way of having some things delivered. He finally decided he should go before Christmas. From the glint in his eyes I believed he wanted to add some festivity to our currently primitive living conditions. For my sake, he didn't need to do anything, but for his own, he did, so I didn't argue. We made a new list, adding a few baby items, lanolin, safety pins, and rubber pants.

Abel left on Christmas Eve right after an extra early breakfast. The cows had been milked, the animals fed, and as much wood as fit was stacked in a corner. I finally thought to ask where the wood had come from, and he told me it was another gift from the Red Cross and would be delivered monthly as long as we needed it. I wondered how long it would take for trees to grow again to the point where we would have our own fuel. We were very low on matches, so I knew while Abel was gone, my main job would be to keep the fire going.

Moosti wasn't so sure of the animals with which he shared a home, so he stayed beside me all his waking hours. He was wonderful company, and I often thought how much Mikko would have enjoyed him. Too often, I broke down as I thought of our little boy.

Abel said he would be home before dark. At the last minute I had sent a letter with him to mail back home. I will never forget the words I wrote:

> *Dear family,*
>
> *Tragedy has come to us. Little Mikko was killed in a fire that also destroyed our farm. A part of my heart will always ache for our little boy. People have been kind to us, and we will survive. A new baby is due soon.*
>
> *Love,*
> *Abel & Eva*

It seemed like such a cold letter, but I knew it had to be sent. I didn't mean to bring pain to my parents or Mumo, but they would want to know. I almost crumpled it up, wanting to rewrite it, but Abel needed to leave, so I sent it with him anyway.

As Abel left, my tears began. I knew I could allow myself the luxury of a good cry without upsetting my husband. I cried and cried until I was completely worn out. I took Moosti in my arms and laid down, wanting to do nothing but sleep. When I awoke, I felt tired but strangely cleansed. Moosti licked my face clear of tears as I took solace in his thick fur and sweet puppy breath.

I spent most of the day making baskets as I kept cozy under a quilt. The day flew by and with six simple baskets made, I realized I hadn't even started supper.

After stoking the fire and starting soup, Moosti and I went outside to relieve ourselves. I was surprised to find the wind blowing and heavy snow coming down. I wondered whether Abel would even make it home that night. Preparing for the worst, I milked our two cows and gave them their nightly water and feed and then returned inside with my pail of milk. Moosti, obviously not liking the snow, shook himself off and laid down close to our stove. It looked like a very good idea, but as I carried water to the lambs, pigs, and chickens, I must have twisted wrong. My lower back began to ache terribly. Within minutes a bout of nausea took over and I found myself vomiting into a bucket. The smell made me even more nauseous so I hurriedly emptied the pail outside and rinsed it with snow. The way I felt, I knew I wouldn't be able to haul water from the river, so I filled all seven of our pails with snow, bringing it in to melt. It wouldn't yield a lot of water but might last until Abel got home. I took a cup of broth from the soup bubbling on the stove but couldn't get it down. With the animals all tended, I felt no guilt in going to bed early. Abel's watch, which he'd left behind for me, chimed seven times just as I was dozing off.

When I again woke it was very dark. Only embers remained of our fire, so I added wood. My stomach was cramping, and I felt miserable but managed to make a trip out to get a good load of wood to last through the night. I wondered where Abel was spending Christmas Eve, glad that he had acquaintances that would take him and our horse in.

As I stacked the wood in the corner, much to my surprise, my water broke, running down my legs and making a puddle on the floor. It was only as I wiped myself off that I realized I was in labor. I'd been certain it would be another month before our baby would arrive, but maybe my long walk home had hurried things along. The reason didn't matter. I had to prepare to give birth, putting a sheet over our bed, finding baby nappies and a blanket, boiling water and finding a knife to sterilize. I worked in automatic, thankful for every instruction Mumo had given me. I had expected to have Abel with me for this birth but had too much to do to spend time fretting. I prayed, asking God to protect the baby and me and to bring back Abel safely. I remembered much of what Mumo had said, about not fighting the pains, but breathing through them. I filled a cup with water, knowing I'd be thirsty. I slipped off all of my clothing but my shift and stockings and slid under our quilt. Moosti, his eyes concerned, laid down beside me. A long while later, as Abel's watch chimed twelve times, I realized it was Christmas Day. I thought of the Christmas story, especially of Mary giving birth in a stable. One of the lambs began bleating, a rarity in the night, and I felt it was its way of comforting me. I wrapped the quilt around me and tried walking in our home, but gave up since there was no room to walk. I poured the melted snow into one pail, stacking the remaining six, and that cleared the floor a bit.

The pains came, growing stronger and longer, just as God had planned, and silent tears ran down my cheeks as I breathed through them. Before I thought it would be possible, I had the urge to push. I leaned against the wall and followed my instincts, pushing out a perfect little boy. I held his helpless body next to my heart, giving thanks for the miracle of birth.

I hadn't expected things to go so fast, so hadn't taken the knife from the water. Somehow with the baby held against me, I fished the knife out of the pan with a fork, managing to keep the blade sterile. The placenta was delivered quickly, and I raised it above the baby to give him the last of the blood he needed before tying the cord twice and cutting it in between. With rags I washed off our baby's beautiful little body causing him to cry loudly. He quickly became contented again as soon as I wrapped him in a blanket and offered my breast. Within moments he was asleep. There was nowhere to lay him down until I thought of the lamb's crib for hay. With him safely sleeping there, I could remove my wet, soiled sheet glad to have an extra one with which to replace it. Our living conditions made everything more difficult, but I managed to clean myself and get into my new flannel nightgown. After water and a little broth, I slipped under our quilt, this time with the baby on one side and Moosti on the other.

It shouldn't have surprised me that once again I fell deeply asleep, waking to the sound of our baby's cries. I sat up to nurse just as the watch chimed four times. The baby sucked eagerly, was re-diapered, re-wrapped, and fell asleep again. It wasn't quite five, the usual time the cows were milked, but feeling wide awake, I got up, fired the stove, and in its warmth dressed myself. Like any other day, the livestock needed food and water, the cows needed to be milked, and the eggs gathered from the hens. With those jobs done and our baby still sleeping, I decided to cook eggs for my breakfast. After eating them and giving Moosti the plate to lick, I looked around for what else to do and decided to go through our clothes, hanging what I could on the hooks and finding places for the rest. I quickly gathered a bundle of soiled clothing, so heated snow to get a pan of water in which to wash them. I didn't want to leave the baby long enough to get water from the river, so continued to gather snow to melt, clearing a path from the sauna/house and lean-to for the cows down towards the river. I started rinse water heating as I rubbed the dirty clothes against a scrub board, feeling satisfaction as the water turned gray. As I emptied the water outside, the sun was rising. The snow had stopped and the wind wasn't blowing, so Abel should be home soon. I spread out the washed clothes as best I could, and realized we badly needed a clothesline in our little space.

Just as I was finishing with our clothes, our neighbors, the Raisanens, came in their horse-drawn sleigh. They had missed us at church the previous night and wanted to make sure we were all right. When they learned he had gone to Cloquet for supplies, they were not surprised that Abel had been delayed by the storm. When Lempi saw that our little babe had arrived, she could barely believe I had delivered him without assistance. We sat on the cot while I nursed the baby, talking about life and miracles. "You sure have Sisu, Eva," she said. "I don't know how you did it."

I told her about Mumo's instruction as she'd delivered Mikko, but she didn't seem impressed. Finally, I was able to say, "It went way beyond Sisu, Lempi. I had God on my side." She just smiled and told me they would leave soon but check back in the morning. Esa carried in more wood and pails of water, so I felt I was in good shape until Abel would return. Lempi also gave me a plate of Christmas cookies, which reminded me of my preparations the previous year. As they left, I hugged them good-bye and thanked them for their thoughtfulness. Lempi asked me what I needed, and when I responded a clothesline, she laughed out loud, saying she thought they could take care of that need.

My early rising, laundry and visiting had left me tired, so I tucked my arm around the baby and immediately fell asleep. I don't know how long I slept, but I awoke when Abel opened the door, carrying bundles. His first words were, "You washed clothes, Eva. Sorry I wasn't here to haul the water. I left the baby on the bed, scooped up Moosti, and set him on the floor to help Abel with his parcels.

"The storm must have come quickly. I'm glad you've made it back."

After two more trips in, Abel took off his long coat, hanging it on a hook and started to sit down on our bed to take off his boots. "Watch out, Abel!" I yelled as I scooped up our little boy into the safety of my arms.

"It looks like you have lots to tell me about, Eva. I think we both need to sit down." And that's what we did, admiring our little boy, who we both felt should be named Johann after our friend who had helped us so much.

As Abel held Johann, examining his long fingers and fine features, he said. "He's beautiful........ but he'll never make up for losing Mikko, will he?"

As he looked at me, I don't think I had ever loved him so much. He understood the depth of our loss and knew our lives could never be the same. Those were the words I said to him and added. "It won't be the same, but we'll make it work. We'll rebuild and do our best."

"You are a wonderful wife, Eva, with great Sisu."

"But even Sisu isn't enough," I smiled gently. "It's our Lord who sustains us."

At that he kissed Johann's forehead and my lips. "Amen," he said.

"Amen," I answered.

Epilogue

Eva and Abel lived in Esko the rest of their lives, rebuilding and adding to their farm, until it grew to be over 300 acres, one of the largest farms in Esko. They raised three boys and were blessed with many grandchildren. Abel died at the age of 72 while Eva lived to be 85. Even during her last years, which she spent at Lakeshore Lutheran Home in Duluth, Eva continued to keep busy knitting for her loved ones.

Acknowledgments

Bible verses are quoted from the King James Bible. Special appreciation is given to the Esko Historical Society, whose publication, <u>Esko's Corner,</u> 2013 was used for background information along with <u>Finns in Minnesota</u> by Arnold R. Alanen, Minnesota Historical Society Press, 2012.

46091365R00070

Made in the USA
Charleston, SC
08 September 2015